CHRISTMAS EVE ON LONESOME
"HELL-FER-SARTAIN"
AND OTHER STORIES

Buck saw the shadowed gesture of an arm, and he cocked his pistol.

CHRISTMAS EVE
ON LONESOME
"HELL-FER-SARTAIN"
AND OTHER STORIES

BY
JOHN *William* FOX, JR.

ILLUSTRATED BY
F. C. YOHN, A. I. KELLER,
W. A. ROGERS AND H. C. RANSOM

15 14

NEW YORK
CHARLES SCRIBNER'S SONS
1910

CONTENTS

CHRISTMAS EVE ON LONESOME AND
OTHER STORIES

PAGE

CHRISTMAS EVE ON LONESOME . . . 3

THE ARMY OF THE CALLAHAN . . . 10

THE PARDON OF BECKY DAY 46

A CRISIS FOR THE GUARD 58

CHRISTMAS NIGHT WITH SATAN . . . 76

"HELL-FER-SARTAIN"

ON HELL-FER-SARTAIN CREEK 99

THROUGH THE GAP 102

A TRICK O' TRADE 106

GRAYSON'S BABY 109

COURTIN' ON CUTSHIN 116

THE MESSAGE IN THE SAND 122

THE SENATOR'S LAST TRADE 125

CONTENTS

PREACHIN' ON KINGDOM-COME . . . 129

THE PASSING OF ABRAHAM SHIVERS . . 134

A PURPLE RHODODENDRON 137

MAN HUNTING IN THE POUND . . . 153

DOWN THE KENTUCKY ON A RAFT . . 173

THROUGH THE BAD BEND 195

TO THE BREAKS OF SANDY 217

ILLUSTRATIONS

Buck saw the shadowed gesture of an arm,
and cocked his pistol . . . . *Frontispiece*

FACING
PAGE

Captain Wells descended with no little majesty
and "biffed" him 20

"Speak up, nigger!" 40

Satan would drop the coin and get a ball for himself 78

" Have you ever searched for a dead man?" . . 168

They took us for the advance guard of a circus . 226

CHRISTMAS EVE ON LONESOME
AND OTHER STORIES

CHRISTMAS EVE ON LONESOME

IT was Christmas Eve on Lonesome. But nobody on Lonesome knew that it was Christmas Eve, although a child of the outer world could have guessed it, even out in those wilds where Lonesome slipped from one lone log cabin high up the steeps, down through a stretch of jungled darkness to another lone cabin at the mouth of the stream.

There was the holy hush in the gray twilight that comes only on Christmas Eve. There were the big flakes of snow that fell as they never fall except on Christmas Eve. There was a snowy man on horseback in a big coat, and with saddle-pockets that might have been bursting with toys for children in the little cabin at the head of the stream.

But not even he knew that it was Christmas Eve. He was thinking of Christmas Eve, but it was of the Christmas Eve of the year before, when he sat in prison with a hundred other men in stripes, and listened to the chaplain talk of peace and good will to all men upon earth, when

3

he had forgotten all men upon earth but one, and had only hatred in his heart for him.

"Vengeance is mine! saith the Lord."

That was what the chaplain had thundered at him. And then, as now, he thought of the enemy who had betrayed him to the law, and had sworn away his liberty, and had robbed him of everything in life except a fierce longing for the day when he could strike back and strike to kill. And then, while he looked back hard into the chaplain's eyes, and now, while he splashed through the yellow mud thinking of that Christmas Eve, Buck shook his head; and then, as now, his sullen heart answered:

"Mine!"

The big flakes drifted to crotch and twig and limb. They gathered on the brim of Buck's slouch hat, filled out the wrinkles in his big coat, whitened his hair and his long mustache, and sifted into the yellow, twisting path that guided his horse's feet.

High above he could see through the whirling snow now and then the gleam of a red star. He knew it was the light from his enemy's window; but somehow the chaplain's voice kept ringing in his ears, and every time he saw the light he couldn't help thinking of the story of the Star that the chaplain told that Christmas Eve, and he dropped his eyes by and by, so as

4

not to see it again, and rode on until the light shone in his face.

Then he led his horse up a little ravine and hitched it among the snowy holly and rhodo-dendrons, and slipped toward the light. There was a dog somewhere, of course; and like a thief he climbed over the low rail-fence and stole through the tall snow-wet grass until he leaned against an apple-tree with the sill of the window two feet above the level of his eyes.

Reaching above him, he caught a stout limb and dragged himself up to a crotch of the tree. A mass of snow slipped softly to the earth. The branch creaked above the light wind; around the corner of the house a dog growled and he sat still.

He had waited three long years and he had ridden two hard nights and lain out two cold days in the woods for this.

And presently he reached out very carefully, and noiselessly broke leaf and branch and twig until a passage was cleared for his eye and for the point of the pistol that was gripped in his right hand.

A woman was just disappearing through the kitchen door, and he peered cautiously and saw nothing but darting shadows. From one cor-ner a shadow loomed suddenly out in human shape. Buck saw the shadowed gesture of an arm, and he cocked his pistol. That shadow was his man, and in a moment he would be in a chair in the chimney corner to smoke his pipe, maybe—his last pipe.

Buck smiled—pure hatred made him smile— but it was mean, a mean and sorry thing to shoot this man in the back, dog though he was; and now that the moment had come a wave of sickening shame ran through Buck. No one of his name had ever done that before; but this man and his people had, and with their own lips they had framed palliation for him. What was fair for one was fair for the other they always said. A poor man couldn't fight money in the courts; and so they had shot from the brush, and that was why they were rich now and Buck was poor —why his enemy was safe at home, and he was out here, homeless, in the apple-tree.

Buck thought of all this, but it was no use. The shadow slouched suddenly and disappeared; and Buck was glad. With a gritting oath between his chattering teeth he pulled his pistol in and thrust one leg down to swing from the tree—he would meet him face to face next day and kill him like a man—and there he hung as rigid as though the cold had suddenly turned him, blood, bones, and marrow, into ice.

The door had opened, and full in the firelight stood the girl who he had heard was dead. He knew now how and why that word was sent him. And now she who had been his sweetheart stood before him—the wife of the man he meant to kill.

Her lips moved—he thought he could tell what she said: "Git up, Jim, git up!" Then she went back.

A flame flared up within him now that must have come straight from the devil's forge. Again the shadows played over the ceiling. His teeth grated as he cocked his pistol, and pointed it down the beam of light that shot into the heart of the apple-tree, and waited.

The shadow of a head shot along the rafters and over the fireplace. It was a madman clutching the butt of the pistol now, and as his eye caught the glinting sight and his heart thumped, there stepped into the square light of the window—a child!

It was a boy with yellow tumbled hair, and he had a puppy in his arms. In front of the fire the little fellow dropped the dog, and they began to play.

"Yap! yap! yap!"

Buck could hear the shrill barking of the fat little dog, and the joyous shrieks of the child as he made his playfellow chase his tail round and round or tumbled him head over heels on the floor. It was the first child Buck had seen for

7

three years; it was *his* child and *hers;* and, in the apple-tree, Buck watched fixedly.

They were down on the floor now, rolling over and over together; and he watched them until the child grew tired and turned his face to the fire and lay still—looking into it. Buck could see his eyes close presently, and then the puppy crept closer, put his head on his playmate's chest, and the two lay thus asleep.

And still Buck looked—his clasp loosening on his pistol and his lips loosening under his stiff mustache—and kept looking until the door opened again and the woman crossed the floor. A flood of light flashed suddenly on the snow, barely touching the snow-hung tips of the apple-tree, and he saw her in the doorway—saw her look anxiously into the darkness—look and listen a long while.

Buck dropped noiselessly to the snow when she closed the door. He wondered what they would think when they saw his tracks in the snow next morning; and then he realized that they would be covered before morning.

As he started up the ravine where his horse was he heard the clink of metal down the road and the splash of a horse's hoofs in the soft mud, and he sank down behind a holly-bush.

Again the light from the cabin flashed out on the snow.

8

" That you, Jim? "

" Yep! "

And then the child's voice: " Has oo dot thum tandy? "

" Yep! "

The cheery answer rang out almost at Buck's ear, and Jim passed death waiting for him behind the bush which his left foot brushed, shaking the snow from the red berries down on the crouching figure beneath.

Once only, far down the dark jungled way, with the underlying streak of yellow that was leading him whither, God only knew—once only Buck looked back. There was the red light gleaming faintly through the moonlit flakes of snow. Once more he thought of the Star, and once more the chaplain's voice came back to him.

" Mine! " saith the Lord.

Just how, Buck could not see with himself in the snow and *him* back there for life with her and the child, but some strange impulse made him bare his head.

" Yourn," said Buck grimly.

But nobody on Lonesome—not even Buck— knew that it was Christmas Eve.

THE ARMY OF THE CALLAHAN

I

THE dreaded message had come. The lank messenger, who had brought it from over Black Mountain, dropped into a chair by the stove and sank his teeth into a great hunk of yellow cheese. " Flitter Bill " Richmond waddled from behind his counter, and out on the little platform in front of his cross-roads store. Out there was a group of earth-stained countrymen, lounging against the rickety fence or swinging on it, their heels clear of the ground, all whittling, chewing, and talking the matter over. All looked up at Bill, and he looked down at them, running his eye keenly from one to another until he came to one powerful young fellow loosely bent over a wagon-tongue. Even on him, Bill's eyes stayed but a moment, and then were lifted higher in anxious thought.

The message had come at last, and the man who brought it had heard it fall from Black Tom's own lips. The " wild Jay-Hawkers of Kaintuck " were coming over into Virginia to

get Flitter Bill's store, for they were mountain
Unionists and Bill was a valley rebel and lawful
prey. It was past belief. So long had he
prospered, and so well, that Bill had come to
feel that he sat safe in the hollow of God's hand.
But he now must have protection—and at once
—from the hand of man.

Roaring Fork sang lustily through the rhododendrons. To the north yawned " the Gap "
through the Cumberland Mountains. " Callahan's Nose," a huge gray rock, showed plain in
the clear air, high above the young foliage, and
under it, and on up the rocky chasm, flashed
Flitter Bill's keen mind, reaching out for help.

Now, from Virginia to Alabama the Southern mountaineer was a Yankee, because the national spirit of 1776, getting fresh impetus in
1812 and new life from the Mexican War, had
never died out in the hills. Most likely it
would never have died out, anyway; for, the
world over, any seed of character, individual or
national, that is once dropped between lofty
summits brings forth its kind, with deathless
tenacity, year after year. Only, in the Kentucky mountains, there were more slaveholders
than elsewhere in the mountains in the South.
These, naturally, fought for their slaves, and
the division thus made the war personal and terrible between the slaveholders who dared to stay

at home, and the Union, " Home Guards " who organized to drive them away. In Bill's little Virginia valley, of course, most of the sturdy farmers had shouldered Confederate muskets and gone to the war. Those who had stayed at home were, like Bill, Confederate in sympathy, but they lived in safety down the valley, while Bill traded and fattened just opposite the Gap, through which a wild road ran over into the wild Kentucky hills. Therein Bill's danger lay; for, just at this time, the Harlan Home Guard under Black Tom, having cleared those hills, were making ready, like the Pict and Scot of olden days, to descend on the Virginia valley and smite the lowland rebels at the mouth of the Gap. Of the " stay-at-homes," and the deserters roundabout, there were many, very many, who would " stand in " with any man who would keep their bellies full, but they were wellnigh worthless even with a leader, and, without a leader, of no good at all. Flitter Bill must find a leader for them, and anywhere than in his own fat self, for a leader of men Bill was not born to be, nor could he see a leader among the men before him. And so, standing there one early morning in the spring of 1865, with uplifted gaze, it was no surprise to him—the coincidence, indeed, became at once one of the articles of perfect faith in his own star—that he should see afar off, a black slouch hat and a jogging gray horse rise above a little knoll that was in line with the mouth of the Gap. At once he crossed his hands over his chubby stomach with a pious sigh, and at once a plan of action began to whirl in his little round head. Before man and beast were in full view the work was done, the hands were unclasped, and Flitter Bill, with a chuckle, had slowly risen, and was waddling back to his desk in the store.

It was a pompous old buck who was bearing down on the old gray horse, and under the slouch hat with its flapping brim—one Mayhall Wells, by name. There were but few strands of gray in his thick blue-black hair, though his years were rounding half a century, and he sat the old nag with erect dignity and perfect ease. His bearded mouth showed vanity immeasurable, and suggested a strength of will that his eyes—the real seat of power—denied, for, while shrewd and keen, they were unsteady. In reality, he was a great coward, though strong as an ox, and whipping with ease every man who could force him into a fight. So that, in the whole man, a sensitive observer would have felt a peculiar pathos, as though nature had given him a desire to be, and no power to become, and had then sent him on his zigzag way, never to dream wherein his trouble lay.

" Mornin', gentle*men*! "

" Mornin', Mayhall! "

All nodded and spoke except Hence Sturgill on the wagon-tongue, who stopped whittling, and merely looked at the big man with narrowing eyes.

Tallow Dick, a yellow slave, appeared at the corner of the store, and the old buck beckoned him to come and hitch his horse. Flitter Bill had reappeared on the stoop with a piece of white paper in his hand. The lank messenger sagged in the doorway behind him, ready to start for home.

" Mornin' *Captain* Wells," said Bill, with great respect. Every man heard the title, stopped his tongue and his knife-blade, and raised his eyes; a few smiled—Hence Sturgill grinned. Mayhall stared, and Bill's left eye closed and opened with lightning quickness in a most portentous wink. Mayhall straightened his shoulders—seeing the game, as did the crowd at once: Flitter Bill was impressing that messenger in case he had some dangerous card up his sleeve.

" *Captain* Wells," Bill repeated significantly, " I'm sorry to say yo' new uniform has not arrived yet. I am expecting it to-morrow." Mayhall toed the line with soldierly promptness.

" Well, I'm sorry to hear that, suh—sorry to

14

hear it, suh," he said, with slow, measured speech. "My men are comin' in fast, and you can hardly realize er—er what it means to an old soldier er—er not to have—er—" And Mayhall's answering wink was portentous.

"My friend here is from over in Kaintucky, and the Harlan Home Gyard over there, he says, is a-making some threats."

Mayhall laughed.

"So I have heerd—so I have heerd." He turned to the messenger. "We shall be ready fer 'em, suh, ready fer 'em with a thousand men —one thousand men, suh, right hyeh in the Gap —right hyeh in the Gap. Let 'em come on—let 'em come on!" Mayhall began to rub his hands together as though the conflict were close at hand, and the mountaineer slapped one thigh heartily. "Good for you! Give 'em hell!" He was about to slap Mayhall on the shoulder and call him "pardner," when Flitter Bill coughed, and Mayhall lifted his chin.

"Captain Wells?" said Bill.

"Captain Wells," repeated Mayhall with a stiff salutation, and the messenger from over Black Mountain fell back with an apologetic laugh. A few minutes later both Mayhall and Flitter Bill saw him shaking his head, as he started homeward toward the Gap. Bill laughed silently, but Mayhall had grown grave. The fun was over and he beckoned Bill inside the store.

"Misto Richmond," he said, with hesitancy and an entire change of tone and manner, "I am afeerd I ain't goin' to be able to pay you that little amount I owe you, but if you can give me a little mo' time——"

"Captain Wells," interrupted Bill slowly, and again Mayhall stared hard at him, "as betwixt friends, as have been pussonal friends fer nigh onto twenty year, I hope you won't mention that little matter to me ag'in—until I mentions it to you."

"But, Misto Richmond, Hence Sturgill out thar says as how he heerd you say that if I didn't pay——"

"*Captain* Wells," interrupted Bill again and again Mayhall stared hard—it was strange that Bill could have formed the habit of calling him "Captain" in so short a time—"yestiddy is not to-day, is it? And to-day is not to-morrow? I axe you—have I said one word about that little matter *to-day?* Well, borrow not from yestiddy nor to-morrow, to make trouble fer to-day. There is other things fer to-day, Captain Wells."

Mayhall turned here.

"Misto Richmond," he said, with great earnestness, "you may not know it, but three times since thet long-legged jay-hawker's been gone you hev plainly—and if my ears do not deceive me, an' they never hev—you have plainly called me ' *Captain* Wells.' I knowed yo' little trick whilst he was hyeh, fer I knowed whut the feller had come to tell ye; but since he's been gone, three times, Misto Richmond——"

" Yes," drawled Bill, with an unction that was strangely sweet to Mayhall's wondering ears, " an' I do it ag'in, *Captain* Wells."

" An' may I axe you," said Mayhall, ruffling a little, " may I axe you—why you——"

" Certainly," said Bill, and he handed over the paper that he held in his hand.

Mayhall took the paper and looked it up and down helplessly—Flitter Bill slyly watching him.

Mayhall handed it back. " If you please, Misto Richmond—I left my specs at home." Without a smile, Bill began. It was an order from the commandant at Cumberland Gap, sixty miles farther down Powell's Valley, authorizing Mayhall Wells to form a company to guard the Gap and to protect the property of Confederate citizens in the valley; and a commission of captaincy in the said company for the said Mayhall Wells. Mayhall's mouth widened to the full stretch of his lean jaws, and, when Bill was through reading, he silently reached for the paper and looked it up and down and over and over, muttering:

" Well—well—well ! " And then he pointed silently to the name that was at the bottom of the paper.

Bill spelled out the name:

" *Jefferson Davis,*" and Mayhall's big fingers trembled as he pulled them away, as though to avoid further desecration of that sacred name.

Then he rose, and a magical transformation began that can be likened—I speak with reverence—to the turning of water into wine. Captain Mayhall Wells raised his head, set his chin well in, and kept it there. He straightened his shoulders, and kept them straight. He paced the floor with a tread that was martial, and once he stopped before the door with his right hand thrust under his breast-pocket, and with wrinkling brow studied the hills. It was a new man —with the water in his blood changed to wine— who turned suddenly on Flitter Bill Richmond:

" I can collect a vehy large force in a vehy few days." Flitter Bill knew that—that he could get together every loafer between the county-seat of Wise and the county-seat of Lee—but he only said encouragingly:

" Good! "

" An' we air to pertect the property—*I am to*

18

pertect the property of the Confederate citizens of the valley—that means *you*, Misto Richmond, and *this store*."

Bill nodded.

Mayhall coughed slightly. "There is one thing in the way, I opine. Whar—I axe you—air we to git somethin' to eat fer my command?" Bill had anticipated this.

"I'll take keer o' that."

Captain Wells rubbed his hands.

"Of co'se, of co'se—you are a soldier and a patriot—you can afford to feed 'em as a slight return fer the pertection I shall give you and yourn."

"Certainly," agreed Bill dryly, and with a prophetic stir of uneasiness.

"Vehy—vehy well. I shall begin *now*, Misto Richmond." And, to Flitter Bill's wonder, the captain stalked out to the stoop, announced his purpose with the voice of an auctioneer, and called for volunteers then and there. There was dead silence for a moment. Then there was a smile here, a chuckle there, an incredulous laugh, and Hence Sturgill, "bully of the Pocket," rose from the wagon-tongue, closed his knife, came slowly forward, and cackled his scorn straight up into the teeth of Captain Mayhall Wells. The captain looked down and began to shed his coat.

" I take it, Hence Sturgill, that you air laughin' at me? "

" I am a-laughin' at *you*, Mayhall Wells,"
he said, contemptuously, but he was surprised at the look on the good-natured giant's
face.

" *Captain* Mayhall Wells, ef you please."

" Plain ole Mayhall Wells," said Hence, and
Captain Wells descended with no little majesty
and " biffed " him.

The delighted crowd rose to its feet and gathered around. Tallow Dick came running from
the barn. It was biff—biff, and biff again, but
not nip and tuck for long. Captain Mayhall
closed in. Hence Sturgill struck the earth like
a Homeric pine, and the captain's mighty arm
played above him and fell, resounding. In
three minutes Hence, to the amazement of the
crowd, roared:

" 'Nough! "

But Mayhall breathed hard and said quietly:
"*Captain* Wells!"

Hence shouted, "Plain ole—" But the captain's huge fist was poised in the air over his face.

" Captain Wells," he growled, and the captain rose and calmly put on his coat, while the
crowd looked respectful, and Hence Sturgill
staggered to one side, as though beaten in spirit,
strength, and wits as well. The captain beck-

Captain Wells descended with no little majesty and "biffed" him.

oned Flitter Bill inside the store. His manner had a distinct savor of patronage.

"Misto Richmond," he said, " I make you— I appoint you, by the authority of Jefferson Davis and the Confederate States of Ameriky, as commissary-gineral of the Army of the Callahan."

"As *what?*" Bill's eyes blinked at the astounding dignity of his commission.

"Gineral Richmond, I shall not repeat them words." And he didn't, but rose and made his way toward his old gray mare. Tallow Dick held his bridle.

"Dick," he said jocosely, " goin' to run away ag'in?" The negro almost paled, and then, with a look at a blacksnake whip that hung on the barn door, grinned.

"No, suh—no, suh—'deed I ain't, suh—no mo'."

Mounted, the captain dropped a three-cent silver piece in the startled negro's hand. Then he vouchsafed the wondering Flitter Bill and the gaping crowd a military salute and started for the yawning mouth of the Gap—riding with shoulders squared and chin well in—riding as should ride the commander of the Army of the Callahan.

Flitter Bill dropped his blinking eyes to the paper in his hand that bore the commission of

Jefferson Davis and the Confederate States of America to Mayhall Wells of Callahan, and went back into his store. He looked at it a long time and then he laughed, but without much mirth.

II

GRASS had little chance to grow for three weeks thereafter under the cowhide boots of Captain Mayhall Wells. When the twentieth morning came over the hills, the mist parted over the Stars and Bars floating from the top of a tall poplar up through the Gap and flaunting brave defiance to Black Tom, his Harlan Home Guard, and all other jay-hawking Unionists of the Kentucky hills. It parted over the Army of the Callahan asleep on its arms in the mouth of the chasm, over Flitter Bill sitting, sullen and dejected, on the stoop of his store; and over Tallow Dick stealing corn bread from the kitchen to make ready for flight that night through the Gap, the mountains, and to the yellow river that was the Mecca of the runaway slave.

At the mouth of the Gap a ragged private stood before a ragged tent, raised a long dinner horn to his lips, and a mighty blast rang through the hills, reveille! And out poured the Army of the Callahan from shack, rock-cave, and coverts of sticks and leaves, with squirrel rifles,

23

Revolutionary muskets, shotguns, clasp-knives, and horse pistols for the duties of the day under Lieutenant Skaggs, tactician, and Lieutenant Boggs, quondam terror of Roaring Fork.

That blast rang down the valley into Flitter Bill's ears and startled him into action. It brought Tallow Dick's head out of the barn door and made him grin.

"Dick!" Flitter Bill's call was sharp and angry.

"Yes, suh!"

"Go tell ole Mayhall Wells that I ain't goin' to send him nary another pound o' bacon an' nary another tin cup o' meal—no, by ——, I ain't."

Half an hour later the negro stood before the ragged tent of the commander of the Army of the Callahan.

"Marse Bill say he ain't gwine to sen' you no mo' rations—no mo'."

"*What!*"

Tallow Dick repeated his message and the captain scowled—mutiny!

"Fetch my hoss!" he thundered.

Very naturally and very swiftly had the trouble come, for straight after the captain's fight with Hence Sturgill there had been a mighty rally to the standard of Mayhall Wells. From

Pigeon's Creek the loafers came—from Roaring Fork, Cracker's Neck, from the Pocket down the valley, and from Turkey Cove. Recruits came so fast, and to such proportions grew the Army of the Callahan, that Flitter Bill shrewdly suggested at once that Captain Wells divide it into three companies and put one up Pigeon's Creek under Lieutenant Jim Skaggs and one on Callahan under Lieutenant Tom Boggs, while the captain, with a third, should guard the mouth of the Gap. Bill's idea was to share with those districts the honor of his commissary-generalship; but Captain Wells crushed the plan like a dried puffball.

"Yes," he said, with fine sarcasm. "What will them Kanetuckians do then? Don't you know, Gineral Richmond? Why, I'll tell you what they'll do. They'll jest swoop down on Lieutenant Boggs and gobble him up. Then they'll swoop down on Lieutenant Skaggs on Pigeon and gobble him up. Then they'll swoop down on me and gobble me up. No, they won't gobble *me* up, but they'll come damn nigh it. An' what kind of a report will I make to Jeff Davis, Gineral Richmond? *Captured in detail,* suh? No, suh. I'll jest keep Lieutenant Boggs and Lieutenant Skaggs close by me, and we'll pitch our camp right here in the Gap whar we can pertect the property of Confederate citizens and be close to our base o' supplies, suh.   That's what I'll do!"

"Gineral Richmond" groaned, and when in the next breath the mighty captain casually inquired if *that uniform of his* had come yet, Flitter Bill's fat body nearly rolled off his chair.

"You will please have it here next Monday," said the captain, with great firmness.   "It is necessary to the proper discipline of my troops." And it was there the following Monday—a regimental coat, gray jeans trousers, and a forage cap that Bill purchased from a passing Morgan raider.   Daily orders would come from Captain Wells to General Flitter Bill Richmond to send up more rations, and Bill groaned afresh when a man from Callahan told how the captain's family was sprucing up on meal and flour and bacon from the captain's camp.   Humiliation followed.   It had never occurred to Captain Wells that being a captain made it incongruous for him to have a "general" under him, until Lieutenant Skaggs, who had picked up a manual of tactics somewhere, cautiously communicated his discovery.   Captain Wells saw the point at once.   There was but one thing to do—to reduce General Richmond to the ranks—and it was done.   Technically, thereafter, the general was purveyor for the Army of the Callahan, but

26

to the captain himself he was—gallingly to the purveyor—simple Flitter Bill.

The strange thing was that, contrary to his usual shrewdness, it should have taken Flitter Bill so long to see that the difference between having his store robbed by the Kentucky jay-hawkers and looted by Captain Wells was the difference between tweedle-dum and tweedle-dee, but, when he did see, he forged a plan of relief at once. When the captain sent down Lieutenant Boggs for a supply of rations, Bill sent the saltiest, rankest bacon he could find, with a message that he wanted to see the great man. As before, when Captain Wells rode down to the store, Bill handed out a piece of paper, and, as before, the captain had left his "specs" at home. The paper was an order that, whereas the distinguished services of Captain Wells to the Confederacy were appreciated by Jefferson Davis, the said Captain Wells was, and is, hereby empowered to duly, and in accordance with the tactics of war, impress what live-stock he shall see fit and determine fit for the good of his command. The news was joy to the Army of the Callahan. Before it had gone the rounds of the camp Lieutenant Boggs had spied a fat heifer browsing on the edge of the woods and ordered her surrounded and driven down. Without another word, when she was close enough, he raised his gun and would have shot her dead in her tracks had he not been arrested by a yell of command and horror from his superior.

"Air you a-goin' to have me cashiered and shot, Lieutenant Boggs, fer violatin' the tick-tacks of war?" roared the captain, indignantly. "Don't you know that I've got to *impress* that heifer accordin' to the rules an' regulations? Git roun' that heifer." The men surrounded her. "Take her by the horns. Now! In the name of Jefferson Davis and the Confederate States of Ameriky, I hereby and hereon do duly impress this heifer for the purposes and use of the Army of the Callahan, so help me God! Shoot her down, Bill Boggs, shoot her down!"

Now, naturally, the soldiers preferred fresh meat, and they got it—impressing cattle, sheep, and hogs, geese, chickens, and ducks, vegetables —nothing escaped the capacious maw of the Army of the Callahan. It was a beautiful idea, and the success of it pleased Flitter Bill mightily, but the relief did not last long. An indignant murmur rose up and down valley and creek bottom against the outrages, and one angry old farmer took a pot-shot at Captain Wells with a squirrel rifle, clipping the visor of his forage cap; and from that day the captain began to call with immutable regularity again on Flitter Bill for bacon and meal. That morning the last straw fell in a demand for a wagon-load of rations to be delivered before noon, and, worn to the edge of his patience, Bill had sent a reckless refusal.   And now he was waiting on the stoop of his store, looking at the mouth of the Gap and waiting for it to give out into the valley Captain Wells and his old gray mare.   And at last, late in the afternoon, there was the captain coming—coming at a swift gallop—and Bill steeled himself for the onslaught like a knight in a joust against a charging antagonist.   The captain saluted stiffly—pulling up sharply and making no move to dismount.

" Purveyor," he said, " Black Tom has just sent word that he's a-comin' over hyeh this week —have you heerd that, purveyor? "   Bill was silent.

" Black Tom says you *air* responsible for the Army of the Callahan.   Have you heerd that, purveyor? "   Still was there silence.

" He says he's a-goin' to hang me to that poplar whar floats them Stars and Bars "—Captain Mayhall Wells chuckled—" an' he says he's a-goin' to hang *you* thar fust, though; have you heerd *that*, purveyor? "

The captain dropped the titular address now, and threw one leg over the pommel of his saddle.

" Flitter Bill Richmond," he said, with great nonchalance, " I axe you—do you prefer that I should disband the Army of the Callahan, or do you not?"

"No."

The captain was silent a full minute, and his face grew stern. "Flitter Bill Richmond, I had no idee o' disbandin' the Army of the Callahan, but do you know what I did aim to do?" Again Bill was silent.

"Well, suh, I'll tell you whut I aim to do. If you don't send them rations I'll have you cashiered for mutiny, an' if Black Tom don't hang you to that air poplar, I'll hang you thar myself, suh; yes, by ——! I will. Dick!" he called sharply to the slave. "Hitch up that air wagon, fill hit full o' bacon and meal, and drive it up thar to my tent. An' be mighty damn quick about it, or I'll hang you, too."

The negro gave a swift glance to his master, and Flitter Bill feebly waved acquiescence.

"Purveyor, I wish you good-day."

Bill gazed after the great captain in dazed wonder (was this the man who had come cringing to him only a few short weeks ago?) and groaned aloud.

But for lucky or unlucky coincidence, how could the prophet ever have gained name and fame on earth?

Captain Wells rode back to camp chuckling—

chuckling with satisfaction and pride; but the
chuckle passed when he caught sight of his tent.
In front of it were his lieutenants and some half
a dozen privates, all plainly in great agitation,
and in the midst of them stood the lank messenger who had brought the first message from
Black Tom, delivering another from the same
source. Black Tom *was* coming, coming sure,
and unless that flag, that " Rebel rag," were
hauled down under twenty-four hours, Black
Tom would come over and pull it down, and to
that same poplar hang " Captain Mayhall an'
his whole damn army." Black Tom might do
it anyhow—just for fun.

While the privates listened the captain
strutted and swore; then he rested his hand on
his hip and smiled with silent sarcasm, and then
swore again—while the respectful lieutenants
and the awed soldiery of the Callahan looked on.
Finally he spoke.

" Ah—when did Black Tom say that? " he
inquired casually.

" Yestiddy mornin'. He said he was goin' to
start over hyeh early this mornin'." The captain whirled.

" What? Then why didn't you git over hyeh
this mornin'? "

" Couldn't git across the river last night."

" Then he's a-comin' to-day? "

" I reckon Black Tom'll be hyeh in about two hours—mebbe he ain't fer away now." The captain was startled.

" Lieutenant Skaggs," he called, sharply, " git yo' men out thar an' draw 'em up in two rows! "

The face of the student of military tactics looked horrified. The captain in his excitement had relaxed into language that was distinctly agricultural, and, catching the look on his subordinate's face, and at the same time the reason for it, he roared, indignantly:

" Air you afeer'd, sir? Git yo' men out, I said, an' march 'em up thar in front of the Gap. Lieutenant Boggs, take ten men an' march at double quick through the Gap, an' defend that poplar with yo' life's blood. If you air overwhelmed by superior numbers, fall back, suh, step by step, until you air re-enforced by Lieutenant Skaggs. If you two air not able to hold the enemy in check, you may count on me an' the Army of the Callahan to grind *him*—" (How the captain, now thoroughly aroused to all the fine terms of war, did roll that technical " him " under his tongue)—" to grind him to pieces ag'in them towerin' rocks, and plunge him in the bilin' waters of Roarin' Fawk. Forward, suh —double quick." Lieutenant Skaggs touched his cap. Lieutenant Boggs looked embarrassed and strode nearer.

" Captain, whar am I goin' to git ten men to face them Kanetuckians? "

" Whar air they goin' to git a off'cer to lead 'em, you'd better say," said the captain, severely, fearing that some of the soldiers had heard the question. " If you air afeer'd, suh "—and then he saw that no one had heard, and he winked— winked with most unmilitary familiarity.

" Air you a good climber, Lieutenant Boggs? " Lieutenant Boggs looked mystified, but he said he was.

" Lieutenant Boggs, I now give you the opportunity to show yo' profound knowledge of the ticktacks of war. You may now be guilty of disobedience of ordahs, and I will not have you court-martialled for the same. In other words, if, after a survey of the situation, you think best—why," the captain's voice dropped to a hoarse whisper, " pull that flag down, Lieutenant Boggs, pull her down."

III

IT was an hour by sun now. Lieutenant Boggs and his devoted band of ten were making their way slowly and watchfully up the mighty chasm—the lieutenant with his hand on his sword and his head bare, and bowed in thought. The Kentuckians were on their way —at that moment they might be riding full speed toward the mouth of Pigeon, where floated the flag. They might gobble him and his command up when they emerged from the Gap. Suppose they caught him up that tree. His command might escape, but *he* would be up there, saving them the trouble of stringing him up. All they would have to do would be to send up after him a man with a rope, and let him drop. That was enough. Lieutenant Boggs called a halt and explained the real purpose of the expedition.

"We will wait here till dark," he said, " so them Kanetuckians can't ketch us, whilst we are climbing that tree."

And so they waited opposite Bee Rock, which was making ready to blossom with purple rhododendrons. And the reserve back in the Gap, under Lieutenant Skaggs, waited. Waited, too, the Army of the Callahan at the mouth of the Gap, and waited restlessly Captain Wells at the door of his tent, and Flitter Bill on the stoop of his store—waited everybody but Tallow Dick, who, in the general confusion, was slipping through the rhododendrons along the bank of Roaring Fork, until he could climb the mountain-side and slip through the Gap high over the army's head.

What could have happened?

When dusk was falling, Captain Wells dispatched a messenger to Lieutenant Skaggs and his reserve, and got an answer; Lieutenant Skaggs feared that Boggs had been captured without the firing of a single shot—but the flag was floating still. An hour later, Lieutenant Skaggs sent another message—he could not see the flag. Captain Wells answered, stoutly:

" Hold yo' own."

And so, as darkness fell, the Army of the Callahan waited in the strain of mortal expectancy as one man; and Flitter Bill waited, with his horse standing saddled in the barn, ready for swift flight. And, as darkness fell, Tallow Dick was cautiously picking his way alongside the steep wall of the Gap toward freedom, and picking it with stealthy caution, foot by foot;

for up there, to this day, big loose rocks mount halfway to the jagged points of the black cliffs, and a careless step would have detached one and sent an avalanche of rumbling stones down to betray him. A single shot rang suddenly out far up through the Gap, and the startled negro sprang forward, slipped, and, with a low, frightened oath, lay still. Another shot followed, and another. Then a hoarse murmur rose, loudened into thunder, and ended in a frightful —boom! One yell rang from the army's throat:

"The Kentuckians! The Kentuckians! The wild, long-haired, terrible Kentuckians!"

Captain Wells sprang into the air.

"My God, they've got a cannon!"

Then there was a martial chorus—the crack of rifle, the hoarse cough of horse-pistol, the roar of old muskets.

"Bing! Bang! Boom! Bing—bing! Bang —bang! Boom—boom! Bing—bang—boom!"

Lieutenant Skaggs and his reserves heard the beat of running feet down the Gap.

"They've gobbled Boggs," he said, and the reserve rushed after him as he fled. The army heard the beat of their coming feet.

"They've gobbled Skaggs," the army said.

Then was there bedlam as the army fled—a crashing through bushes—a splashing into the river, the rumble of mule wagons, yells of terror, swift flying shapes through the pale moonlight. Flitter Bill heard the din as he stood by his barn door.

"They've gobbled the army," said Flitter Bill, and he, too, fled like a shadow down the valley.

Nature never explodes such wild and senseless energy as when she lets loose a mob in a panic. With the army, it was each man for himself and devil take the hindmost; and the flight of the army was like a flight from the very devil himself. Lieutenant Boggs, whose feet were the swiftest in the hills, outstripped his devoted band. Lieutenant Skaggs, being fat and slow, fell far behind his reserve, and dropped exhausted on a rock for a moment to get his breath. As he rose, panting, to resume flight, a figure bounded out of the darkness behind him, and he gathered it in silently and went with it to the ground, where both fought silently in the dust until they rolled into the moonlight and each looked the other in the face.

"That you, Jim Skaggs?"

"That you, Tom Boggs?"

Then the two lieutenants rose swiftly, but a third shape bounded into the road—a gigantic figure—Black Tom! With a startled yell they gathered him in—one by the waist, the other about the neck, and, for a moment, the terrible

Kentuckian—it could be none other—swung the two clear of the ground, but the doughty lieutenants hung to him. Boggs trying to get his knife and Skaggs his pistol, and all went down in a heap.

"I surrender—I surrender!" It was the giant who spoke, and at the sound of his voice both men ceased to struggle, and, strange to say, no one of the three laughed.

"Lieutenant Boggs," said Captain Wells, thickly, "take yo' thumb out o' my mouth. Lieutenant Skaggs, leggo my leg an' stop bitin' me."

"Sh—sh—sh—" said all three.

The faint swish of bushes as Lieutenant Boggs's ten men scuttled into the brush behind them—the distant beat of the army's feet getting fainter ahead of them, and then silence—dead, dead silence.

"Sh—sh—sh!"

* * * * *

With the red streaks of dawn Captain Mayhall Wells was pacing up and down in front of Flitter Bill's store, a gaping crowd about him, and the shattered remnants of the army drawn up along Roaring Fork in the rear. An hour later Flitter Bill rode calmly in.

"I stayed all night down the valley," said Flitter Bill. "Uncle Jim Richmond was sick.

I hear you had some trouble last night, Captain Wells." The captain expanded his chest.

"Trouble!" he repeated, sarcastically. And then he told how a charging horde of daredevils had driven him from camp with overwhelming numbers and one piece of artillery; how he had rallied the army and fought them back, foot by foot, and put them to fearful rout; how the army had fallen back again just when the Kentuckians were running like sheep, and how he himself had stayed in the rear with Lieutenant Boggs and Lieutenant Skaggs, "to cover their retreat, suh," and how the purveyor, if he would just go up through the Gap, would doubtless find the cannon that the enemy had left behind in their flight It was just while he was thus telling the tale for the twentieth time that two figures appeared over the brow of the hill and drew near—Hence Sturgill on horseback and Tallow Dick on foot.

"I ketched this nigger in my corn-fiel' this mornin'," said Hence, simply, and Flitter Bill glared, and without a word went for the blacksnake ox-whip that hung by the barn door.

For the twenty-first time Captain Wells started his tale again, and with every pause that he made for breath Hence cackled scorn.

"An', Hence Sturgill, ef you will jus' go up

in the Gap you'll find a cannon, captured, suh, by me an' the Army of the Callahan, an'——"

"Cannon!" Hence broke in. "Speak up, nigger!" And Tallow Dick spoke up—grinning:

"I done it!"

"What!" shouted Flitter Bill.

"I kicked a rock loose climbin' over Callahan's Nose."

Bill dropped his whip with a chuckle of pure ecstasy. Mayhall paled and stared. The crowd roared, the Army of the Callahan grinned, and Hence climbed back on his horse.

"Mayhall Wells," he said, "plain ole Mayhall Wells, I'll see you on Couht Day. I ain't got time now."

And he rode away.

"Speak up, nigger."

IV

THAT day Captain Mayhall Wells and the Army of the Callahan were in disrepute. Next day the awful news of Lee's surrender came. Captain Wells refused to believe it, and still made heroic effort to keep his shattered command together. Looking for recruits on Court Day, he was twitted about the rout of the army by Hence Sturgill, whose long-coveted chance to redeem himself had come. Again, as several times before, the captain declined to fight—his health was essential to the general well-being— but Hence laughed in his face, and the captain had to face the music, though the heart of him was gone.

He fought well, for he was fighting for his all, and he knew it. He could have whipped with ease, and he did whip, but the spirit of the thoroughbred was not in Captain Mayhall Wells. He had Sturgill down, but Hence sank his teeth into Mayhall's thigh while Mayhall's hands grasped his opponent's throat. The captain had only to squeeze, as every rough-and-tumble fighter knew, and endure his pain until

Hence would have to give in. But Mayhall was not built to endure. He roared like a bull as soon as the teeth met in his flesh, his fingers relaxed, and to the disgusted surprise of everybody he began to roar with great distinctness and agony:

" 'Nough! 'Nough!"

The end was come, and nobody knew it better than Mayhall Wells. He rode home that night with hands folded on the pommel of his saddle and his beard crushed by his chin against his breast. For the last time, next morning he rode down to Flitter Bill's store. On the way he met Parson Kilburn and for the last time Mayhall Wells straightened his shoulders and for one moment more resumed his part: perhaps the parson had not heard of his fall.

" Good-mornin', parsing," he said, pleasantly. " Ah—where have you been?" The parson was returning from Cumberland Gap, whither he had gone to take the oath of allegiance.

" By the way, I have something here for you which Flitter Bill asked me to give you. He said it was from the commandant at Cumberland Gap."

" Fer me?" asked the captain—hope springing anew in his heart. The parson handed him a letter. Mayhall looked at it upside down.

" If you please, parsing," he said, handing it back, " I hev left my specs at home."

The parson read that, whereas Captain Wells had been guilty of grave misdemeanors while in command of the Army of the Callahan, he should be arrested and court-martialled for the same, or be given the privilege of leaving the county in twenty-four hours. Mayhall's face paled a little and he stroked his beard.

" Ah—does anybody but you know about this ordah, parsing? "

" Nobody."

" Well, if you will do me the great favor, parsing, of not mentioning it to nary a living soul—as fer me and my ole gray hoss and my household furniture—we'll be in Kanetuck afore daybreak to-morrow mornin'! " And he was.

But he rode on just then and presented himself for the last time at the store of Flitter Bill. Bill was sitting on the stoop in his favorite posture. And in a moment there stood before him plain Mayhall Wells—holding out the order Bill had given the parson that day.

" Misto Richmond," he said, " I have come to tell you good-by."

Now just above the selfish layers of fat under Flitter Bill's chubby hands was a very kind heart. When he saw Mayhall's old manner and heard the old respectful way of address, and felt the dazed helplessness of the big, beaten man, the heart thumped.

"I am sorry about that little amount I owe you; I think I'll be able shortly—" But Bill cut him short. Mayhall Wells, beaten, disgraced, driven from home on charge of petty crimes, of which he was undoubtedly guilty, but for which Bill knew he himself was responsible —Mayhall on his way into exile and still persuading himself and, at that moment, almost persuading him that he meant to pay that little debt of long ago—was too much for Flitter Bill, and he proceeded to lie—lying with deliberation and pleasure.

"Captain Wells," he said—and the emphasis on the title was balm to Mayhall's soul—"you have protected me in time of war, an' you air welcome to yo' uniform an' you air welcome to that little debt. Yes," he went on, reaching down into his pocket and pulling out a roll of bills, "I tender you in payment for that same protection the regular pay of a officer in the Confederate service"—and he handed out the army pay for three months in Confederate greenbacks—"an' five dollars in money of the United States, of which I an', doubtless, you, suh, air true and loyal citizens. Captain Wells, I bid you good-by an' I wish ye well—I wish ye well."

From the stoop of his store Bill watched the captain ride away, drooping at the shoulders, and with his hands folded on the pommel of his saddle—his dim blue eyes misty, the jaunty forage cap a mockery of his iron-gray hair, and the flaps of his coat fanning either side like mournful wings.

And Flitter Bill muttered to himself:

" Atter he's gone long enough fer these things to blow over, I'm going to bring him back and give him another chance—yes, damme if I don't git him back."

And Bill dropped his remorseful eye to the order in his hand. Like the handwriting of the order that lifted Mayhall like magic into power, the handwriting of this order, that dropped him like a stone—was Flitter Bill's own.

THE PARDON OF BECKY DAY

THE missionary was young and she was from the North. Her brows were straight, her nose was rather high, and her eyes were clear and gray. The upper lip of her little mouth was so short that the teeth just under it were never quite concealed. It was the mouth of a child and it gave the face, with all its strength and high purpose, a peculiar pathos that no soul in that little mountain town had the power to see or feel. A yellow mule was hitched to the rickety fence in front of her and she stood on the stoop of a little white frame-house with an elm switch between her teeth and gloves on her hands, which were white and looked strong. The mule wore a man's saddle, but no matter— the streets were full of yellow pools, the mud was ankle-deep, and she was on her way to the sick-bed of Becky Day.

There was a flood that morning. All the preceding day the rains had drenched the high slopes unceasingly. That night, the rain-clear forks of the Kentucky got yellow and rose high,

46

and now they crashed together around the town and, after a heaving conflict, started the river on one quivering, majestic sweep to the sea.

Nobody gave heed that the girl rode a mule or that the saddle was not her own, and both facts she herself quickly forgot. This half log, half frame house on a corner had stood a siege once. She could yet see bullet holes about the door. Through this window, a revenue officer from the Blue Grass had got a bullet in the shoulder from a garden in the rear. Standing in the post-office door only just one month before, she herself had seen children scurrying like rabbits through the back-yard fences, men running silently here and there, men dodging into doorways, fire flashing in the street and from every house—and not a sound but the crack of pistol and Winchester; for the mountain men deal death in all the terrible silence of death. And now a preacher with a long scar across his forehead had come to the one little church in the place and the fervor of religion was struggling with feudal hate for possession of the town. To the girl, who saw a symbol in every mood of the earth, the passions of these primitive people were like the treacherous streams of the uplands —now quiet as sunny skies and now clashing together with but little less fury and with much more noise. And the roar of the flood above

the wind that late afternoon was the wrath of
the Father, that with the peace of the Son so
long on earth, such things still could be. Once
more trouble was threatening and that day even
she knew that trouble might come, but she rode
without fear, for she went when and where she
pleased as any woman can, throughout the Cumberland, without insult or harm.

At the end of the street were two houses that
seemed to front each other with unmistakable
enmity. In them were two men who had
wounded each other only the day before, and
who that day would lead the factions, if the old
feud broke loose again. One house was close
to the frothing hem of the flood—a log-hut with
a shed of rough boards for a kitchen—the home
of Becky Day.

The other was across the way and was framed
and smartly painted. On the steps sat a woman
with her head bare and her hands under her
apron—widow of the Marcum whose death
from a bullet one month before had broken the
long truce of the feud. A groaning curse was
growled from the window as the girl drew near,
and she knew it came from a wounded Marcum
who had lately come back from the West to
avenge his brother's death.

"Why don't you go over to see your neighbor?" The girl's clear eyes gave no hint that

she knew—as she well did—the trouble between the houses, and the widow stared in sheer amazement, for mountaineers do not talk with strangers of the quarrels between them.

" I have nothin' to do with such as her," she said, sullenly; " she ain't the kind——"

" Don't! " said the girl, with a flush, " she's dying."

" *Dyin'?* "

" Yes." With the word the girl sprang from the mule and threw the reins over the pale of the fence in front of the log-hut across the way. In the doorway she turned as though she would speak to the woman on the steps again, but a tall man with a black beard appeared in the low door of the kitchen-shed.

" How is your—how is Mrs. Day? "

" Mighty puny this mornin'—Becky is."

The girl slipped into the dark room. On a disordered, pillowless bed lay a white face with eyes closed and mouth slightly open. Near the bed was a low wood fire. On the hearth were several thick cups filled with herbs and heavy fluids and covered with tarpaulin, for Becky's " man " was a teamster. With a few touches of the girl's quick hands, the covers of the bed were smooth, and the woman's eyes rested on the girl's own cloak. With her own handkerchief she brushed the death-damp from the forehead that already seemed growing cold. At her first touch, the woman's eyelids opened and dropped together again. Her lips moved, but no sound came from them.

In a moment the ashes disappeared, the hearth was clean and the fire was blazing. Every time the girl passed the window she saw the widow across the way staring hard at the hut. When she took the ashes into the street, the woman spoke to her.

" I can't go to see Becky—she hates me."

" With good reason."

The answer came with a clear sharpness that made the widow start and redden angrily; but the girl walked straight to the gate, her eyes ablaze with all the courage that the mountain woman knew and yet with another courage to which the primitive creature was a stranger—a courage that made the widow lower her own eyes and twist her hands under her apron.

" I want you to come and ask Becky to forgive you."

The woman stared and laughed.

" Forgive me? Becky forgive me? She wouldn't—an' I don't want her—" She could not look up into the girl's eyes; but she pulled a pipe from under the apron, laid it down with a trembling hand and began to rock slightly.

The girl leaned across the gate.

"Look at me!" she said, sharply. The woman raised her eyes, swerved them once, and then in spite of herself, held them steady.

"Listen! Do you want a dying woman's curse?"

It was a straight thrust to the core of a superstitious heart and a spasm of terror crossed the woman's face. She began to wring her hands.

"Come on!" said the girl, sternly, and turned, without looking back, until she reached the door of the hut, where she beckoned and stood waiting, while the woman started slowly and helplessly from the steps, still wringing her hands. Inside, behind her, the wounded Marcum, who had been listening, raised himself on one elbow and looked after her through the window.

"She can't come in—not while I'm in here."

The girl turned quickly. It was Dave Day, the teamster, in the kitchen door, and his face looked blacker than his beard.

"Oh!" she said, simply, as though hurt, and then with a dignity that surprised her, the teamster turned and strode towards the back door.

"But I can git out, I reckon," he said, and he never looked at the widow who had stopped, frightened, at the gate.

"Oh, I can't—I *can't!*" she said, and her voice broke; but the girl gently pushed her to the door, where she stopped again, leaning against the lintel. Across the way, the wounded Marcum, with a scowl of wonder, crawled out of his bed and started painfully to the door. The girl saw him and her heart beat fast.

Inside, Becky lay with closed eyes. She stirred uneasily, as though she felt some hated presence, but her eyes stayed fast, for the presence of Death in the room was stronger still.

"Becky!" At the broken cry, Becky's eyes flashed wide and fire broke through the haze that had gathered in them.

"I want ye ter fergive me, Becky."

The eyes burned steadily for a long time. For two days she had not spoken, but her voice came now, as though from the grave.

"You!" she said, and, again, with torturing scorn, "You!" And then she smiled, for she knew why her enemy was there, and her hour of triumph was come. The girl moved swiftly to the window—she could see the wounded Marcum slowly crossing the street, pistol in hand.

"What'd I ever do to you?"

"Nothin', Becky, nothin'."

Becky laughed harshly. "You can tell the truth—can't ye—to a dyin' woman?"

"Fergive me, Becky!"

A scowling face, tortured with pain, was thrust into the window.

" Sh-h ! " whispered the girl, imperiously, and the man lifted his heavy eyes, dropped one elbow on the window-sill and waited.

" You tuk Jim from me ! "

The widow covered her face with her hands, and the Marcum at the window—brother to Jim, who was dead—lowered at her, listening keenly.

" An' you got him by lyin' 'bout me. You tuk him by lyin' 'bout me—didn't ye? Didn't ye? " she repeated, fiercely, and her voice would have wrung the truth from a stone.

" Yes—Becky—yes ! "

" You hear? " cried Becky, turning her eyes to the girl.

" You made him believe an' made ever'body, you could, believe that I was—was *bad*." Her breath got short, but the terrible arraignment went on.

" You started this war. My brother wouldn't 'a' shot Jim Marcum if it hadn't been fer you. You killed Jim—your own husband—an' you killed *me*. An' now you want me to fergive you—you ! " She raised her right hand as though with it she would hurl the curse behind her lips, and the widow, with a cry, sprang for the bony fingers, catching them in her own hand and falling over on her knees at the bedside.

" Don't, Becky, don't—don't—*don't!* "

There was a slight rustle at the back window. At the other, a pistol flashed into sight and dropped again below the sill. Turning, the girl saw Dave's bushy black head—he, too, with one elbow on the sill and the other hand out of sight.

" Shame! " she said, looking from one to the other of the two men, who had learned, at last, the bottom truth of the feud; and then she caught the sick woman's other hand and spoke quickly.

" Hush, Becky," she said; and at the touch of her hand and the sound of her voice, Becky looked confusedly at her and let her upraised hand sink back to the bed. The widow stared swiftly from Jim's brother, at one window, to Dave Day at the other, and hid her face on her arms.

" Remember, Becky—how can you expect forgiveness in another world, unless you forgive in this? "

The woman's brow knitted and she lay quiet. Like the widow who held her hand, the dying woman believed, with never the shadow of a doubt, that somewhere above the stars, a living God reigned in a heaven of never-ending happiness; that somewhere beneath the earth a personal devil gloated over souls in eternal torture; that whether she went above, or below, hung solely on her last hour of contrition; and that in heaven or hell she would know those whom she might meet as surely as she had known them on earth. By and by her face softened and she drew a long breath.

" Jim was a good man," she said. And then after a moment:

" An' I was a good woman "—she turned her eyes towards the girl—" until Jim married *her*. I didn't keer after that." Then she got calm, and while she spoke to the widow, she looked at the girl.

"Will you git up in church an' say before ever'body that you knew I was *good* when you said I was bad—that you lied about me?"

" Yes—yes." Still Becky looked at the girl, who stooped again.

" She will, Becky, I know she will. Won't you forgive her and leave peace behind you? Dave and Jim's brother are here—make them shake hands. Won't you—won't you?" she asked, turning from one to the other.

Both men were silent.

" Won't you?" she repeated, looking at Jim's brother.

" I've got nothin' agin Dave. I always thought that she "—he did not call his brother's wife by name—caused all this trouble. I've nothin' agin Dave."

The girl turned. " Won't you, Dave? "

" I'm waitin' to hear whut Becky says."

Becky was listening, though her eyes were closed. Her brows knitted painfully. It was a hard compromise that she was asked to make between mortal hate and a love that was more than mortal, but the Plea that has stood between them for nearly twenty centuries prevailed, and the girl knew that the end of the feud was nigh.

Becky nodded.

" Yes, I fergive her, an' I want 'em to shake hands."

But not once did she turn her eyes to the woman whom she forgave, and the hand that the widow held gave back no answering pressure. The faces at the windows disappeared, and she motioned for the girl to take her weeping enemy away.

She did not open her eyes when the girl came back, but her lips moved and the girl bent above her.

" I know whar Jim is."

From somewhere outside came Dave's cough, and the dying woman turned her head as though she were reminded of something she had quite forgotten. Then, straightway, she forgot again.

The voice of the flood had deepened. A smile came to Becky's lips—a faint, terrible

56

smile of triumph. The girl bent low and, with a startled face, shrank back.

"*An' I'll—git—thar—first.*"

With that whisper went Becky's last breath, but the smile was there, even when her lips were cold.

A CRISIS FOR THE GUARD

THE tutor was from New England, and he was precisely what passes, with Southerners, as typical. He was thin, he wore spectacles, he talked dreamy abstractions, and he looked clerical. Indeed, his ancestors had been clergymen for generations, and, by nature and principle, he was an apostle of peace and a noncombatant. He had just come to the Gap—a cleft in the Cumberland Mountains—to prepare two young Blue Grass Kentuckians for Harvard. The railroad was still thirty miles away, and he had travelled mule-back through mudholes, on which, as the joke ran, a traveller was supposed to leave his card before he entered and disappeared—that his successor might not unknowingly press him too hard. I do know that, in those mudholes, mules were sometimes drowned. The tutor's gray mule fell over a bank with him, and he would have gone back had he not feared what was behind more than anything that was possible ahead. He was mud-bespattered, sore, tired and dispirited when he reached the Gap, but still plucky and full of business. He wanted

58

to see his pupils at once and arrange his schedule. They came in after supper, and I had to laugh when I saw his mild eyes open. The boys were only fifteen and seventeen, but each had around him a huge revolver and a belt of cartridges, which he unbuckled and laid on the table after shaking hands. The tutor's shining glasses were raised to me for light. I gave it: my brothers had just come in from a little police duty, I explained. Everybody was a policeman at the Gap, I added; and, naturally, he still looked puzzled; but he began at once to question the boys about their studies, and, in an hour, he had his daily schedule mapped out and submitted to me. I had to cover my mouth with my hand when I came to one item—" Exercise: a walk of half an hour every Wednesday afternoon between five and six "—for the younger, known since at Harvard as the colonel, and known then at the Gap as the Infant of the Guard, winked most irreverently. As he had just come back from a ten-mile chase down the valley on horseback after a bad butcher, and as either was apt to have a like experience any and every day, I was not afraid they would fail to get exercise enough; so I let that item of the tutor pass.

The tutor slept in my room that night, and my four brothers, the eldest of whom was a lieutenant on the police guard, in a room across the hallway. I explained to the tutor that there was much lawlessness in the region; that we "foreigners" were trying to build a town, and that, to ensure law and order, we had all become volunteer policemen. He seemed to think it was most interesting.

About three o'clock in the morning a shrill whistle blew, and, from habit, I sprang out of bed. I had hardly struck the floor when four pairs of heavy boots thundered down the stairs just outside the door, and I heard a gasp from the startled tutor. He was bolt upright in bed, and his face in the moonlight was white with fear.

"Wha—wha—what's that?"

I told him it was a police whistle and that the boys were answering it. Everybody jumped when he heard a whistle, I explained; for nobody in town was permitted to blow one except a policeman. I guessed there would be enough men answering that whistle without me, however, and I slipped back into bed.

"Well," he said; and when the boys lumbered upstairs again and one shouted through the door, "All right!" the tutor said again with emphasis: "Well!"

Next day there was to be a political gathering at the Gap. A Senator was trying to lift himself by his own boot-straps into the Governor's chair. He was going to make a speech, there would be a big and unruly crowd, and it would be a crucial day for the Guard. So, next morning, I suggested to the tutor that it would be unwise for him to begin work with his pupils that day, for the reason that he was likely to be greatly interrupted and often. He thought, however, he would like to begin. He did begin, and within half an hour Gordon, the town sergeant, thrust his head inside the door and called the colonel by name.

"Come on," he said; "they're going to try that d—n butcher." And seeing from the tutor's face that he had done something dreadful, he slammed the door in apologetic confusion. The tutor was law-abiding, and it was the law that called the colonel, and so the tutor let him go—nay, went with him and heard the case. The butcher had gone off on another man's horse —the man owed him money, he said, and the only way he could get his money was to take the horse as security. But the sergeant did not know this, and he and the colonel rode after him, and the colonel, having the swifter horse, but not having had time to get his own pistol, took the sergeant's and went ahead. He fired quite close to the running butcher twice, and the butcher thought it wise to halt. When he saw the child who had captured him he was speechless, and he

got off his horse and cut a big switch to give the
colonel a whipping, but the doughty Infant drew
down on him again and made him ride, foaming
with rage, back to town. The butcher was good-
natured at the trial, however, and the tutor heard
him say, with a great guffaw:

"An' I *do* believe the d—n little fool would
'a' shot me."

Once more the tutor looked at the pupil whom
he was to lead into the classic halls of Harvard,
and once more he said:

"Well!"

People were streaming into town now, and I
persuaded the tutor that there was no use for
him to begin his studies again. He said he would
go fishing down the river and take a swim. He
would get back in time to hear the speaking in
the afternoon. So I got him a horse, and he
came out with a long cane fishing-pole and a pair
of saddle-bags. I told him that he must watch
the old nag or she would run away with him,
particularly when he started homeward. The
tutor was not much of a centaur. The horse
started as he was throwing the wrong leg over
his saddle, and the tutor clamped his rod under
one arm, clutching for the reins with both hands
and kicking for his stirrups with both feet. The
tip of the limber pole beat the horse's flank gently as she struck a trot, and smartly as she struck

into a lope, and so with arms, feet, saddle-pockets, and fishing-rod flapping towards different
points of the compass, the tutor passed out of
sight over Poplar Hill on a dead run.

As soon as he could get over a fit of laughter
and catch his breath, the colonel asked:

"Do you know what he had in those saddle-
pockets?"

"No."

"A bathing suit," he shouted; and he went off
again.

Not even in a primeval forest, it seemed,
would the modest Puritan bare his body to the
mirror of limpid water and the caress of mountain air.

*   *   *   *   *

The trouble had begun early that morning,
when Gordon, the town sergeant, stepped from
his door and started down the street with no little self-satisfaction. He had been arraying himself for a full hour, and after a tub-bath and a
shave he stepped, spick and span, into the street
with his head steadily held high, except when he
bent it to look at the shine of his boots, which
was the work of his own hands, and of which
he was proud. As a matter of fact, the sergeant felt that he looked just as he particularly
wanted to look on that day—his best. Gordon

was a native of Wise, but that day a girl was coming from Lee, and he was ready for her.

Opposite the Intermont, a pistol-shot cracked from Cherokee Avenue, and from habit he started that way. Logan, the captain of the Guard—the leading lawyer in that part of the State—was ahead of him however, and he called to Gordon to follow. Gordon ran in the grass along the road to keep those boots out of the dust. Somebody had fired off his pistol for fun and was making tracks for the river. As they pushed the miscreant close, he dashed into the river to wade across. It was a very cold morning, and Gordon prayed that the captain was not going to be such a fool as to follow the fellow across the river. He should have known better.

" In with you," said the captain quietly, and the mirror of the shining boots was dimmed, and the icy water chilled the sergeant to the knees and made him so mad that he flashed his pistol and told the runaway to halt, which he did in the middle of the stream. It was Richards, the tough from " the Pocket," and, as he paid his fine promptly, they had to let him go. Gordon went back, put on his everyday clothes and got his billy and his whistle and prepared to see the maid from Lee when his duty should let him. As a matter of fact, he saw her but once, and then he was not made happy.

The people had come in rapidly—giants from the Crab Orchard, mountaineers from through the Gap, and from Cracker's Neck and Thunderstruck Knob; Valley people from Little Stone Gap, from the furnace site and Bum Hollow and Wildcat, and people from Lee, from Turkey Cove, and from the Pocket—the much-dreaded Pocket—far down in the river hills.

They came on foot and on horseback, and left their horses in the bushes and crowded the streets and filled the saloon of one Jack Woods—who had the cackling laugh of Satan and did not like the Guard, for good reasons, and whose particular pleasure was to persuade some customer to stir up a hornet's nest of trouble. From the saloon the crowd moved up towards the big spring at the foot of Imboden Hill, where, under beautiful trunk-mottled beeches, was built the speakers' platform.

Precisely at three o'clock the local orator, much flurried, rose, ran his hand through his long hair and looked in silence over the crowd.

" Fellow citizens! There's beauty in the stars of night and in the glowin' orb of day. There's beauty in the rollin' meadow and in the quiet stream. There's beauty in the smilin' valley and in the everlastin' hills. Therefore, fellow citizens—THEREFORE, fellow citizens, allow me to introduce to you the future Governor of these

65

United States — Senator William Bayhone."
And he sat down with such a beatific smile of
self-satisfaction that a fiend would not have had
the heart to say he had not won.

Now, there are wandering minstrels yet in the
Cumberland Hills. They play fiddles and go
about making up "ballets" that involve local
history. Sometimes they make a pretty good
verse—this, for instance, about a feud:

> The death of these two men
>   Caused great trouble in our land.
> Caused men to leave their families
>   And take the parting hand.
> Retaliation, still at war,
>   May never, never cease.
> I would that I could only see
>   Our land once more at peace.

There was a minstrel out in the crowd, and
pretty soon he struck up his fiddle and his lay,
and he did not exactly sing the virtues of Billy
Bayhone. Evidently some partisan thought he
ought, for he smote him on the thigh with the
toe of his boot and raised such a stir as a rude
stranger might had he smitten a troubadour in
Arthur's Court. The crowd thickened and
surged, and four of the Guard emerged with the
fiddler and his assailant under arrest. It was as
though the Valley were a sheet of water straight-

way and the fiddler the dropping of a stone, for the ripple of mischief started in every direction. It caught two mountaineers on the edge of the crowd, who for no particular reason thumped each other with their huge fists, and were swiftly led away by that silent Guard. The operation of a mysterious force was in the air and it puzzled the crowd. Somewhere a whistle would blow, and, from this point and that, a quiet, well-dressed young man would start swiftly toward it. The crowd got restless and uneasy, and, by and by, experimental and defiant. For in that crowd was the spirit of Bunker Hill and King's Mountain. It couldn't fiddle and sing; it couldn't settle its little troubles after the good old fashion of fist and skull; it couldn't charge up and down the streets on horseback if it pleased; it couldn't ride over those puncheon sidewalks; it couldn't drink openly and without shame; and, Shades of the American Eagle and the Stars and Stripes, it couldn't even yell No wonder, like the heathen, it raged. What did these blanked " furriners " have against them anyhow? They couldn't run *their* country—not much.

Pretty soon there came a shrill whistle far down-town — then another and another. It sounded ominous, indeed, and it was, being a signal of distress from the Infant of the Guard, who stood before the door of Jack Woods's saloon with his pistol levelled on Richards, the tough from the Pocket, the Infant, standing there with blazing eyes, alone and in the heart of a gathering storm.

Now the chain of lawlessness that had tightened was curious and significant. There was the tough and his kind—lawless, irresponsible and possible in any community. There was the farm-hand who had come to town with the wild son of his employer—an honest, law-abiding farmer. Came, too, a friend of the farmer who had not yet reaped the crop of wild oats sown in his youth. Whiskey ran all into one mould. The farm-hand drank with the tough, the wild son with the farm-hand, and the three drank together, and got the farmer's unregenerate friend to drink with them; and he and the law-abiding farmer himself, by and by, took a drink for old time's sake. Now the cardinal command of rural and municipal districts all through the South is, " Forsake not your friend ": and it does not take whiskey long to make friends. Jack Woods had given the tough from the Pocket a whistle.

" You dassen't blow it," said he.

Richards asked why, and Jack told him. Straightway the tough blew the whistle, and when the little colonel ran down to arrest him he laughed and resisted, and the wild son and the farm-hand and Jack Woods showed an

68

inclination to take his part. So, holding his "drop" on the tough with one hand, the Infant blew vigorously for help with the other.

Logan, the captain, arrived first—he usually arrived first—and Gordon, the sergeant, was by his side—Gordon was always by his side. He would have stormed a battery if the captain had led him, and the captain would have led him— alone—if he thought it was his duty. Logan was as calm as a stage hero at the crisis of a play. The crowd had pressed close.

"Take that man," he said sharply, pointing to the tough whom the colonel held covered, and two men seized him from behind.

The farm-hand drew his gun.

"No, you don't!" he shouted.

"Take *him*," said the captain quietly; and he was seized by two more and disarmed.

It was then that Sturgeon, the wild son, ran up.

"You can't take that man to jail," he shouted with an oath, pointing at the farm-hand.

The captain waved his hand. "And *him!*"

As two of the Guard approached, Sturgeon started for his gun. Now, Sturgeon was Gordon's blood cousin, but Gordon levelled his own pistol. Sturgeon's weapon caught in his pocket, and he tried to pull it loose. The moment he succeeded Gordon stood ready to fire. Twice

69

the hammer of the sergeant's pistol went back almost to the turning-point, and then, as he pulled the trigger again, Macfarlan, first lieutenant, who once played lacrosse at Yale, rushed, parting the crowd right and left, and dropped his billy lightly three times—right, left and right—on Sturgeon's head. The blood spurted, the head fell back between the bully's shoulders, his grasp on his pistol loosened, and he sank to his knees. For a moment the crowd was stunned by the lightning quickness of it all. It was the first blow ever struck in that country with a piece of wood in the name of the law.

"Take 'em on, boys," called the captain, whose face had paled a little, though he seemed as cool as ever.

And the boys started, dragging the three struggling prisoners, and the crowd, growing angrier and angrier, pressed close behind, a hundred of them, led by the farmer himself, a giant in size, and beside himself with rage and humiliation. Once he broke through the guard line and was pushed back. Knives and pistols began to flash now everywhere, and loud threats and curses rose on all sides—the men should not be taken to jail. The sergeant, dragging Sturgeon, looked up into the blazing eyes of a girl on the sidewalk, Sturgeon's sister—the maid from Lee. The sergeant groaned. Logan gave some order just then to the Infant, who ran ahead, and by the time the Guard with the prisoners had backed to a corner there were two lines of Guards drawn across the street. The first line let the prisoners and their captors through, closed up behind, and backed slowly towards the corner, where it meant to stand.

It was very exciting there. Winchesters and shotguns protruded from the line threateningly, but the mob came on as though it were going to press through, and determined faces blenched with excitement, but not with fear. A moment later, the little colonel and the Guards on either side of him were jabbing at men with cocked Winchesters. At that moment it would have needed but one shot to ring out to have started an awful carnage; but not yet was there a man in the mob—and that is the trouble with mobs— who seemed willing to make a sacrifice of himself that the others might gain their end. For one moment they halted, cursing and waving their pistols, preparing for a charge; and in that crucial moment the tutor from New England came like a thunderbolt to the rescue. Shrieks of terror from children, shrieks of outraged modesty from women, rent the air down the street where the huddled crowd was rushing right and left in wild confusion, and, through the parting crowd, the tutor flew into sight on horseback, bareheaded, barefooted, clad in a gaudily striped bathing suit, with his saddle-pockets flapping behind him like wings. Some mischievous mountaineers, seeing him in his bathing suit on the point of a rock up the river, had joyously taken a pot-shot or two at him, and the tutor had mounted his horse and fled. But he came as welcome and as effective as an emissary straight from the God of Battles, though he came against his will, for his old nag was frantic and was running away. Men, women and children parted before him, and gaping mouths widened as he passed. The impulse of the crowd ran faster than his horse, and even the enraged mountaineers in amazed wonder sprang out of his way, and, far in the rear, a few privileged ones saw the frantic horse plunge towards his stable, stop suddenly, and pitch his mottled rider through the door and mercifully out of sight. Human purpose must give way when a pure miracle comes to earth to baffle it. It gave way now long enough to let the oaken doors of the calaboose close behind tough, farm-hand, and the farmer's wild son. The line of Winchesters at the corner quietly gave way. The power of the Guard was established, the backbone of the opposition broken; henceforth, the work for law and order was to be easy compared with what it had been. Up at the big spring under the beeches sat the disgusted orator of the day and the disgusted Senator, who, seriously, was quite sure that the Guard, being composed of Democrats, had taken this way to shatter his campaign.

*   *   *   *   *

Next morning, in court, the members of the Guard acted as witnesses against the culprits. Macfarlan stated that he had struck Sturgeon over the head to save his life, and Sturgeon, after he had paid his fine, said he would prefer being shot to being clubbed to death, and he bore dangerous malice for a long time, until he learned what everybody else knew, that Macfarlan always did what he thought he ought, and never spoke anything but the literal truth, whether it hurt friend, foe or himself.

After court, Richards, the tough, met Gordon, the sergeant, in the road. " Gordon," he said, " you swore to a ——— lie about me a while ago."

" How do you want to fight? " asked Gordon.

" Fair! "

" Come on "; and Gordon started for the town limits across the river, Richards following on horseback. At a store, Gordon unbuckled his belt and tossed his pistol and his police badge inside. Jack Woods, seeing this, followed, and the Infant, seeing Woods, followed too. The law was law, but this affair was personal, and would be settled without the limits of law and local obligation. Richards tried to talk to Gordon, but the sergeant walked with his head down, as though he could not hear—he was too enraged to talk.

While Richards was hitching his horse in the bushes the sergeant stood on the bank of the river with his arms folded and his chin swinging from side to side. When he saw Richards in the open he rushed for him like a young bull that feels the first swelling of his horns. It was not a fair, stand-up, knock-down English fight, but a Scotch tussle, in which either could strike, kick, bite or gouge. After a few blows they clinched and whirled and fell, Gordon on top— with which advantage he began to pound the tough from the Pocket savagely. Woods made as if to pull him off, but the Infant drew his pistol. "Keep off!"

"He's killing him!" shouted Woods, halting.

"Let him holler 'Enough,' then," said the Infant.

"He's killing him!" shouted Woods.

"Let Gordon's friends take him off, then," said the Infant. "Don't *you* touch him."

And it was done. Richards was senseless and speechless—he really couldn't shout "Enough." But he was content, and the day left a very satisfactory impression on him and on his friends.

If they misbehaved in town they would be arrested: that was plain. But it was also plain
that if anybody had a personal grievance against
one of the Guard he could call him out of the
town limits and get satisfaction, after the way of
his fathers. There was nothing personal at all
in the attitude of the Guard towards the out-
siders; which recognition was a great stride toward mutual understanding and final high re-
gard.

All that day I saw that something was troubling the tutor from New England. It was the
Moral Sense of the Puritan at work, I supposed,
and, that night, when I came in with a new supply of " billies " and gave one to each of my
brothers, the tutor looked up over his glasses and
cleared his throat.

" Now," said I to myself, " we shall catch it
hot on the savagery of the South and the bar-
barous Method of keeping it down "; but before
he had said three words the colonel looked as
though he were going to get up and slap the little dignitary on the back—which would have
created a sensation indeed.

" Have you an extra one of those—those
——"

" Billies? " I said, wonderingly.

" Yes. I—I believe I shall join the Guard
myself," said the tutor from New England.

75

CHRISTMAS NIGHT WITH SATAN

NO night was this in Hades with solemn-eyed Dante, for Satan was only a woolly little black dog, and surely no dog was ever more absurdly misnamed. When Uncle Carey first heard that name, he asked gravely:

"Why, Dinnie, where in h——," Uncle Carey gulped slightly, "did you get him?" And Dinnie laughed merrily, for she saw the fun of the question, and shook her black curls.

"He didn't come f'um *that place.*"

Distinctly Satan had not come from that place. On the contrary, he might by a miracle have dropped straight from some Happy Hunting-ground, for all the signs he gave of having touched pitch in this or another sphere. Nothing human was ever born that was gentler, merrier, more trusting or more lovable than Satan. That was why Uncle Carey said again gravely that he could hardly tell Satan and his little mistress apart. He rarely saw them apart, and as both had black tangled hair and bright black eyes; as one awoke every morning with a happy smile and the other with a jolly bark; as they played all day like wind-shaken shadows and each won every heart at first sight—the likeness was really rather curious. I have always believed that Satan made the spirit of Dinnie's house, orthodox and severe though it was, almost kindly toward his great namesake. I know I have never been able, since I knew little Satan, to think old Satan as bad as I once painted him, though I am sure the little dog had many pretty tricks that the "old boy" doubtless has never used in order to amuse his friends.

"Shut the door, Saty, please." Dinnie would say, precisely as she would say it to Uncle Billy, the butler, and straightway Satan would launch himself at it—bang! He never would learn to close it softly, for Satan liked that—bang!

If you kept tossing a coin or marble in the air, Satan would keep catching it and putting it back in your hand for another throw, till you got tired. Then he would drop it on a piece of rag carpet, snatch the carpet with his teeth, throw the coin across the room and rush for it like mad, until he got tired. If you put a penny on his nose, he would wait until you counted, one—two—*three!* Then he would toss it up himself and catch it. Thus, perhaps, Satan grew to love Mammon right well, but for another and better reason than that he liked simply to throw it around—as shall now be made plain.

A rubber ball with a hole in it was his favorite plaything, and he would take it in his mouth and rush around the house like a child, squeezing it to make it whistle. When he got a new ball, he would hide his old one away until the new one was the worse worn of the two, and then he would bring out the old one again. If Dinnie gave him a nickel or a dime, when they went down-town, Satan would rush into a store, rear up on the counter where the rubber balls were kept, drop the coin, and get a ball for himself. Thus, Satan learned finance. He began to hoard his pennies, and one day Uncle Carey found a pile of seventeen under a corner of the carpet. Usually he carried to Dinnie all coins that he found in the street, but he showed one day that he was going into the ball-business for himself. Uncle Carey had given Dinnie a nickel for some candy, and, as usual, Satan trotted down the street behind her. As usual, Satan stopped before the knick-knack shop.

"Tum on, Saty," said Dinnie. Satan reared against the door as he always did, and Dinnie said again:

"Tum on, Saty." As usual, Satan dropped to his haunches, but what was unusual, he failed to bark. Now Dinnie had got a new ball for Satan only that morning, so Dinnie stamped her foot.

Satan would drop the coin and get a ball for himself.

"I tell you to tum on, Saty." Satan never moved. He looked at Dinnie as much as to say:

"I have never disobeyed you before, little mistress, but this time I have an excellent reason for what must seem to you very bad manners—" and being a gentleman withal, Satan rose on his haunches and begged.

"You're des a pig, Saty," said Dinnie, but with a sigh for the candy that was not to be, Dinnie opened the door, and Satan, to her wonder, rushed to the counter, put his forepaws on it, and dropped from his mouth a dime. Satan had found that coin on the street. He didn't bark for change, nor beg for two balls, but he had got it in his woolly little head, somehow, that in that store a coin meant a ball, though never before nor afterward did he try to get a ball for a penny.

Satan slept in Uncle Carey's room, for of all people, after Dinnie, Satan loved Uncle Carey best. Every day at noon he would go to an upstairs window and watch the cars come around the corner, until a very tall, square-shouldered young man swung to the ground, and down Satan would scamper—yelping—to meet him at the gate. If Uncle Carey, after supper and when Dinnie was in bed, started out of the house, still in his business clothes, Satan would leap out

79

before him, knowing that he too might be allowed to go; but if Uncle Carey had put on black clothes that showed a big, dazzling shirt-front, and picked up his high hat, Satan would sit perfectly still and look disconsolate; for as there were no parties or theatres for Dinnie, so there were none for him. But no matter how late it was when Uncle Carey came home, he always saw Satan's little black nose against the window-pane and heard his bark of welcome.

After intelligence, Satan's chief trait was lovableness—nobody ever knew him to fight, to snap at anything, or to get angry; after lovableness, it was politeness. If he wanted something to eat, if he wanted Dinnie to go to bed, if he wanted to get out of the door, he would beg—beg prettily on his haunches, his little red tongue out and his funny little paws hanging loosely. Indeed, it was just because Satan was so little less than human, I suppose, that old Satan began to be afraid he might have a soul. So the wicked old namesake with the Hoofs and Horns laid a trap for little Satan, and, as he is apt to do, he began laying it early—long, indeed, before Christmas.

When Dinnie started to kindergarten that autumn, Satan found that there was one place where he could never go. Like the lamb, he could not go to school; so while Dinnie was away, Satan began to make friends. He would bark, " Howdy-do? " to every dog that passed his gate. Many stopped to rub noses with him through the fence—even Hugo the mastiff, and nearly all, indeed, except one strange-looking dog that appeared every morning at precisely nine o'clock and took his stand on the corner. There he would lie patiently until a funeral came along, and then Satan would see him take his place at the head of the procession; and thus he would march out to the cemetery and back again. Nobody knew where he came from nor where he went, and Uncle Carey called him the " funeral dog " and said he was doubtless looking for his dead master. Satan even made friends with a scrawny little yellow dog that followed an old drunkard around—a dog that, when his master fell in the gutter, would go and catch a policeman by the coat-tail, lead the officer to his helpless master, and spend the night with him in jail.

By and by Satan began to slip out of the house at night, and Uncle Billy said he reckoned Satan had " jined de club "; and late one night, when he had not come in, Uncle Billy told Uncle Carey that it was " powerful slippery and he reckoned they'd better send de kerridge after him "—an innocent remark that made Uncle Carey send a boot after the old butler, who fled chuckling down the stairs, and left Uncle Carey chuckling in his room.

Satan had " jined de club "—the big club—and no dog was too lowly in Satan's eyes for admission; for no priest ever preached the brotherhood of man better than Satan lived it—both with man and dog.   And thus he lived it that Christmas night—to his sorrow.

Christmas Eve had been gloomy—the gloomiest of Satan's life.   Uncle Carey had gone to a neighboring town at noon.   Satan had followed him down to the station, and when the train started, Uncle Carey had ordered him to go home. Satan took his time about going home, not knowing it was Christmas Eve.   He found strange things happening to dogs that day.   The truth was, that policemen were shooting all dogs found that were without a collar and a license, and every now and then a bang and a howl somewhere would stop Satan in his tracks.   At a little yellow house on the edge of town he saw half a dozen strange dogs in a kennel, and every now and then a negro would lead a new one up to the house and deliver him to a big man at the door, who, in return, would drop something into the negro's hand. While Satan waited, the old drunkard came along with his little dog at his heels, paused before the door, looked a moment at his faithful follower, and went slowly on. Satan little knew the old drunkard's temptation, for in that yellow house kind-hearted people had offered fifteen cents for each dog brought to them, without a license, that they might mercifully put it to death, and fifteen cents was the precise price for a drink of good whiskey. Just then there was another bang and another howl somewhere, and Satan trotted home to meet a calamity. Dinnie was gone. Her mother had taken her out in the country to Grandmother Dean's to spend Christmas, as was the family custom, and Mrs. Dean would not wait any longer for Satan; so she told Uncle Billy to bring him out after supper.

"Ain't you 'shamed o' yo'self—suh—?" said the old butler, "keepin' me from ketchin' Christmas gifts dis day?"

Uncle Billy was indignant, for the negroes begin at four o'clock in the afternoon of Christmas Eve to slip around corners and jump from hiding places to shout "Christmas Gif'—Christmas Gif'"; and the one who shouts first gets a gift. No wonder it was gloomy for Satan—Uncle Carey, Dinnie, and all gone, and not a soul but Uncle Billy in the big house. Every few minutes he would trot on his little black legs upstairs and downstairs, looking for his mistress. As dusk came on, he would every now and then howl plaintively. After begging his supper, and while Uncle Billy was hitching up a horse in the stable, Satan went out in the yard and lay with his nose between the close panels of the fence— quite heart-broken. When he saw his old friend, Hugo, the mastiff, trotting into the gaslight, he began to bark his delight frantically. The big mastiff stopped and nosed his sympathy through the fence for a moment and walked slowly on, Satan frisking and barking along inside. At the gate Hugo stopped, and raising one huge paw, playfully struck it. The gate flew open, and with a happy yelp Satan leaped into the street. The noble mastiff hesitated as though this were not quite regular. He did not belong to the club, and he didn't know that Satan had ever been away from home after dark in his life. For a moment he seemed to wait for Dinnie to call him back as she always did, but this time there was no sound, and Hugo walked majestically on, with absurd little Satan running in a circle about him. On the way they met the " funeral dog," who glanced inquiringly at Satan, shied from the mastiff, and trotted on. On the next block the old drunkard's yellow cur ran across the street, and after interchanging the compliments of the season, ran back after his staggering mas- ter. As they approached the railroad track a strange dog joined them, to whom Hugo paid no attention. At the crossing another new acquaintance bounded toward them. This one—a half-breed shepherd—was quite friendly, and he received Satan's advances with affable condescension. Then another came and another, and little Satan's head got quite confused. They were a queer-looking lot of curs and half-breeds from the negro settlement at the edge of the woods, and though Satan had little experience, his instincts told him that all was not as it should be, and had he been human he would have wondered very much how they had escaped the carnage that day. Uneasy, he looked around for Hugo; but Hugo had disappeared. Once or twice Hugo had looked around for Satan, and Satan paying no attention, the mastiff trotted on home in disgust. Just then a powerful yellow cur sprang out of the darkness over the railroad track, and Satan sprang to meet him, and so nearly had the life scared out of him by the snarl and flashing fangs of the new-comer that he hardly had the strength to shrink back behind his new friend, the half-breed shepherd.

A strange thing then happened. The other dogs became suddenly quiet, and every eye was on the yellow cur. He sniffed the air once or twice, gave two or three peculiar low growls, and all those dogs except Satan lost the civilization of centuries and went back suddenly to the time

when they were wolves and were looking for a
leader. The cur was Lobo for that little pack,
and after a short parley, he lifted his nose high
and started away without looking back, while the
other dogs silently trotted after him. With a
mystified yelp, Satan ran after them. The cur
did not take the turnpike, but jumped the fence
into a field, making his way by the rear of houses,
from which now and then another dog would
slink out and silently join the band. Every one
of them Satan nosed most friendlily, and to his
great joy the funeral dog, on the edge of the
town, leaped into their midst. Ten minutes
later the cur stopped in the midst of some woods,
as though he would inspect his followers. Plainly, he disapproved of Satan, and Satan kept out
of his way. Then he sprang into the turnpike
and the band trotted down it, under flying black
clouds and shifting bands of brilliant moonlight.
Once, a buggy swept past them. A familiar
odor struck Satan's nose, and he stopped for a
moment to smell the horse's tracks; and right
he was, too, for out at her grandmother's Dinnie
refused to be comforted, and in that buggy was
Uncle Billy going back to town after him.

Snow was falling. It was a great lark for
Satan. Once or twice, as he trotted along, he
had to bark his joy aloud, and each time the big
cur gave him such a fierce growl that he feared

thereafter to open his jaws. But he was happy for all that, to be running out into the night with such a lot of funny friends and not to know or care where he was going. He got pretty tired presently, for over hill and down hill they went, at that unceasing trot, trot, trot! Satan's tongue began to hang out. Once he stopped to rest, but the loneliness frightened him and he ran on after them with his heart almost bursting. He was about to lie right down and die, when the cur stopped, sniffed the air once or twice, and with those same low growls, led the marauders through a rail fence into the woods, and lay quietly down. How Satan loved that soft, thick grass, all snowy that it was! It was almost as good as his own bed at home. And there they lay—how long, Satan never knew, for he went to sleep and dreamed that he was after a rat in the barn at home; and he yelped in his sleep, which made the cur lift his big yellow head and show his fangs. The moving of the half-breed shepherd and the funeral dog waked him at last, and Satan got up. Half crouching, the cur was leading the way toward the dark, still woods on top of the hill, over which the Star of Bethlehem was lowly sinking, and under which lay a flock of the gentle creatures that seemed to have been almost sacred to the Lord of that Star. They were in sore need of a watchful shepherd now. Satan was stiff and chilled, but he was rested and had had his sleep, and he was just as ready for fun as he always was. He didn't understand that sneaking. Why they didn't all jump and race and bark as he wanted to, he couldn't see; but he was too polite to do otherwise than as they did, and so he sneaked after them; and one would have thought he knew, as well as the rest, the hellish mission on which they were bent.

Out of the woods they went, across a little branch, and there the big cur lay flat again in the grass. A faint bleat came from the hill-side beyond, where Satan could see another woods—and then another bleat, and another. And the cur began to creep again, like a snake in the grass; and the others crept too, and little Satan crept, though it was all a sad mystery to him. Again the cur lay still, but only long enough for Satan to see curious, fat, white shapes above him—and then, with a blood-curdling growl, the big brute dashed forward. Oh, there was fun in them after all! Satan barked joyfully. Those were some new playmates—those fat, white, hairy things up there; and Satan was amazed when, with frightened snorts, they fled in every direction. But this was a new game, perhaps, of which he knew nothing, and as did the rest, so did Satan. He picked out one of the white things and fled barking after it. It was a little fellow that he was after, but little as he was, Satan might never have caught up, had not the sheep got tangled in some brush. Satan danced about him in mad glee, giving him a playful nip at his wool and springing back to give him another nip, and then away again. Plainly, he was not going to bite back, and when the sheep struggled itself tired and sank down in a heap, Satan came close and licked him, and as he was very warm and woolly, he lay down and snuggled up against him for awhile, listening to the turmoil that was going on around him. And as he listened, he got frightened.

If this was a new game it was certainly a very peculiar one—the wild rush, the bleats of terror, gasps of agony, and the fiendish growls of attack and the sounds of ravenous gluttony. With every hair bristling, Satan rose and sprang from the woods—and stopped with a fierce tingling of the nerves that brought him horror and fascination. One of the white shapes lay still before him. There was a great steaming red splotch on the snow, and a strange odor in the air that made him dizzy; but only for a moment. Another white shape rushed by. A tawny streak followed, and then, in a patch of moonlight, Satan saw the yellow cur with his teeth fastened in the throat of his moaning playmate.

Like lightning Satan sprang at the cur, who tossed him ten feet away and went back to his awful work. Again Satan leaped, but just then a shout rose behind him, and the cur leaped too as though a bolt of lightning had crashed over him, and, no longer noticing Satan or sheep, began to quiver with fright and slink away. Another shout rose from another direction— another from another.

"Drive 'em into the barn-yard!" was the cry.

Now and then there was a fearful bang and a howl of death-agony, as some dog tried to break through the encircling men, who yelled and cursed as they closed in on the trembling brutes that slunk together and crept on; for it is said, every sheep-killing dog knows his fate if caught, and will make little effort to escape. With them went Satan, through the barn-yard gate, where they huddled in a corner—a shamed and terrified group. A tall overseer stood at the gate.

"Ten of 'em!" he said grimly.

He had been on the lookout for just such a tragedy, for there had recently been a sheep-killing raid on several farms in that neighborhood, and for several nights he had had a lantern hung out on the edge of the woods to scare the dogs away; but a drunken farm-hand had neglected his duty that Christmas Eve.

"Yassuh, an' dey's jus' sebenteen dead sheep out dar," said a negro.

"Look at the little one," said a tall boy who looked like the overseer; and Satan knew that he spoke of him.

"Go back to the house, son," said the overseer, "and tell your mother to give you a Christmas present I got for you yesterday." With a glad whoop the boy dashed away, and in a moment dashed back with a brand-new .32 Winchester in his hand.

The dark hour before dawn was just breaking on Christmas Day. It was the hour when Satan usually rushed upstairs to see if his little mistress was asleep. If he were only at home now, and if he only had known how his little mistress was weeping for him amid her playthings and his—two new balls and a brass-studded collar with a silver plate on which was his name, Satan Dean; and if Dinnie could have seen him now, her heart would have broken; for the tall boy raised his gun. There was a jet of smoke, a sharp, clean crack, and the funeral dog started on the right way at last toward his dead master. Another crack, and the yellow cur leaped from the ground and fell kicking. Another crack and another, and with each crack a dog tumbled, until little Satan sat on his haunches amid the writhing pack, alone. His time was now come. As the rifle was raised, he heard up at the big house the cries of children; the popping of fire-crackers; tooting of horns and whistles and loud shouts of " Christmas Gif', Christmas Gif'! " His little heart beat furiously. Perhaps he knew just what he was doing; perhaps it was the accident of habit; most likely Satan simply wanted to go home— but when that gun rose, Satan rose too, on his haunches, his tongue out, his black eyes steady and his funny little paws hanging loosely—and begged! The boy lowered the gun.

" Down, sir! " Satan dropped obediently, but when the gun was lifted again, Satan rose again, and again he begged.

" Down, I tell you! " This time Satan would not down, but sat begging for his life. The boy turned.

" Papa, I can't shoot that dog." Perhaps Satan had reached the stern old overseer's heart. Perhaps he remembered suddenly that it was Christmas. At any rate, he said gruffly:

" Well, let him go."

" Come here, sir! " Satan bounded toward the tall boy, frisking and trustful and begged again.

" Go home, sir! "

Satan needed no second command. Without a sound he fled out the barn-yard, and, as he swept under the front gate, a little girl ran out of the front door of the big house and dashed down the steps, shrieking:

"Saty! Saty! Oh, Saty!" But Satan never heard. On he fled, across the crisp fields, leaped the fence and struck the road, lickety-split! for home, while Dinnie dropped sobbing in the snow.

"Hitch up a horse, quick," said Uncle Carey, rushing after Dinnie and taking her up in his arms. Ten minutes later, Uncle Carey and Dinnie, both warmly bundled up, were after flying Satan. They never caught him until they reached the hill on the outskirts of town, where was the kennel of the kind-hearted people who were giving painless death to Satan's four-footed kind, and where they saw him stop and turn from the road. There was divine providence in Satan's flight for one little dog that Christmas morning; for Uncle Carey saw the old drunkard staggering down the road without his little companion, and a moment later, both he and Dinnie saw Satan nosing a little yellow cur between the palings. Uncle Carey knew the little cur, and while Dinnie was shrieking for Satan, he was saying under his breath:

"Well, I swear!—I swear!—I swear!" And while the big man who came to the door was putting Satan into Dinnie's arms, he said, sharply:

" Who brought that yellow dog here?" The man pointed to the old drunkard's figure turning a corner at the foot of the hill.

" I thought so; I thought so. He sold him to you for—for a drink of whiskey."

The man whistled.

" Bring him out. I'll pay his license."

So back went Satan and the little cur to Grandmother Dean's—and Dinnie cried when Uncle Carey told her why he was taking the little cur along. With her own hands she put Satan's old collar on the little brute, took him to the kitchen, and fed him first of all. Then she went into the breakfast-room.

" Uncle Billy," she said severely, " didn't I tell you not to let Saty out?"

" Yes, Miss Dinnie," said the old butler.

" Didn't I tell you I was goin' to whoop you if you let Saty out?"

" Yes, Miss Dinnie."

Miss Dinnie pulled forth from her Christmas treasures a toy riding-whip and the old darky's eyes began to roll in mock terror.

" I'm sorry, Uncle Billy, but I des got to whoop you a little."

" Let Uncle Billy off, Dinnie," said Uncle Carey, " this is Christmas."

"All wite," said Dinnie, and she turned to Satan.

In his shining new collar and innocent as a cherub, Satan sat on the hearth begging for his breakfast.

"HELL–FER–SARTAIN"

TO
MY BROTHER
JAMES

ON HELL–FER–SARTAIN CREEK

THAR was a dancin'-party Christmas night on "Hell fer Sartain." Jes tu'n up the fust crick beyond the bend thar, an' climb onto a stump, an' holler about *once*, an' you'll see how the name come. Stranger, hit's *hell* fer sartain! Well, Rich Harp was thar from the headwaters, an' Harve Hall toted Nance Osborn clean across the Cumberlan'. Fust one ud swing Nance, an' then t'other. Then they'd take a pull out'n the same bottle o' moonshine, an'——fust one an' then t'other—they'd swing her agin. An' Abe Shivers a-settin' thar by the fire a-bitin' his thumbs!

Well, things was sorter whoopin', when somebody ups an' tells Harve that Rich had said somep'n' agin Nance an' him, an' somebody ups an' tells Rich that Harve had said somep'n' agin Nance an' *him*. In a minute, stranger, hit was like two wild-cats in thar. Folks got 'em parted, though, but thar was no more a-swingin' of Nance that night. Harve toted her back over the Cumberlan', an' Rich's kinsfolks tuk him up "Hell fer Sartain"; but Rich got loose, an' lit out lickety-split fer Nance Osborn's. He knowed Harve lived too fer over Black Mountain to go home that night, an' he rid right across the river an' up to Nance's house, an' hollered for Harve. Harve poked his head out'n the loft—he knowed whut was wanted—an' Harve says, " Uh, come in hyeh an' go to bed. Hit's too late! " An' Rich seed him a-gapin' like a chicken, an' in he walked, stumblin' might' nigh agin the bed whar Nance was a-layin', listenin' an' not sayin' a word.

Stranger, them two fellers slept together plum frien'ly, an' they et together plum frien'ly next mornin', an' they sa'ntered down to the grocery plum frien'ly. An' Rich says, " Harve," says he, " let's have a drink." " All right, Rich," says Harve. An' Rich says, " Harve," says he, " you go out'n that door an' I'll go out'n this door." " All right, Rich," says Harve, an' out they walked, steady, an' thar was two shoots shot, an' Rich an' Harve both drapped, an' in ten minutes they was stretched out on Nance's bed an' Nance was a-lopin' away fer the yarb doctor.

The gal nussed 'em both plum faithful. Rich didn't hev much to say, an' Harve didn't hev much to say. Nance was sorter quiet, an' Nance's mammy, ole Nance, jes grinned. Folks come in to ax atter 'em right peart. Abe Shivers come cl'ar 'cross the river—powerful frien'ly

—an' ever' time Nance ud walk out to the fence with him. One time she didn't come back, an' ole Nance fotched the boys thar dinner, an' ole Nance fotched thar supper, an' then Rich he axed whut was the matter with young Nance. An' ole Nance jes snorted. Atter a while Rich says: "Harve," says he, "who tol' you that I said that word agin you an' Nance?" "Abe Shivers," says Harve. "An' who tol' you," says Harve, "that I said that word agin Nance an' *you?*" "Abe Shivers," says Rich. An' both says, "Well, damn me!" An' Rich tu'ned right over an' begun pullin' straws out'n the bed. He got two out, an' he bit one off, an' he says: "Harve," says he, "I reckon we better draw fer him. The shortes' gits him." An' they drawed. Well, nobody ever knowed which got the short-es' straw, stranger, but——

Thar'll be a dancin'-party comin' Christmas night on "Hell fer Sartain." Rich Harp 'll be thar from the headwaters. Harve Hall's a-goin' to tote the Widder Shivers clean across the Cumberlan'. Fust one 'll swing Nance, an' then t'other. Then they'll take a pull out'n the same bottle o' moonshine, an'—fust one an' then t'other—they'll swing her agin, jes the same. *Abe* won't be thar. He's a-settin' by a bigger fire, I reckon (ef he ain't in it), a-bitin' his thumbs!

THROUGH THE GAP

WHEN thistles go adrift, the sun sets down the valley between the hills; when snow comes, it goes down behind the Cumberland and streams through a great fissure that people call the Gap. Then the last light drenches the parson's cottage under Imboden Hill, and leaves an after-glow of glory on a majestic heap that lies against the east. Sometimes it spans the Gap with a rainbow.

Strange people and strange tales come through this Gap from the Kentucky hills. Through it came these two, late one day—a man and a woman—afoot. I met them at the footbridge over Roaring Fork.

" Is thar a preacher anywhar aroun' hyeh? " he asked. I pointed to the cottage under Imboden Hill. The girl flushed slightly and turned her head away with a rather unhappy smile. Without a word, the mountaineer led the way towards town. A moment more and a half-breed Malungian passed me on the bridge and followed them.

At dusk the next day I saw the mountaineer

chopping wood at a shanty under a clump of rhododendron on the river-bank. The girl was cooking supper inside. The day following he was at work on the railroad, and on Sunday, after church, I saw the parson. The two had not been to him. Only that afternoon the mountaineer was on the bridge with another woman, hideously rouged and with scarlet ribbons fluttering from her bonnet. Passing on by the shanty, I saw the Malungian talking to the girl. She apparently paid no heed to him until, just as he was moving away, he said something mockingly, and with a nod of his head back towards the bridge. She did not look up even then, but her face got hard and white, and, looking back from the road, I saw her slipping through the bushes into the dry bed of the creek, to make sure that what the half-breed told her was true.

The two men were working side by side on the railroad when I saw them again, but on the first pay-day the doctor was called to attend the Malungian, whose head was split open with a shovel. I was one of two who went out to arrest his assailant, and I had no need to ask who he was. The mountaineer was a devil, the foreman said, and I had to club him with a pistol-butt before he would give in. He said he would get even with me; but they all say that, and I paid no attention to the threat. For a week he was kept in the calaboose, and when I passed the shanty just after he was sent to the county-seat for trial, I found it empty. The Malungian, too, was gone. Within a fortnight the mountaineer was in the door of the shanty again. Having no accuser, he had been discharged. He went back to his work, and if he opened his lips I never knew. Every day I saw him at work, and he never failed to give me a surly look. Every dusk I saw him in his doorway, waiting, and I could guess for what. It was easy to believe that the stern purpose in his face would make its way through space and draw her to him again. And she did come back one day. I had just limped down the mountain with a sprained ankle. A crowd of women was gathered at the edge of the woods, looking with all their eyes to the shanty on the river-bank. The girl stood in the door-way. The mountaineer was coming back from work with his face down.

"He hain't seed her yit," said one. "He's goin' to kill her shore. I tol' her he would. She said she reckoned he would, but she didn't keer."

For a moment I was paralyzed by the tragedy at hand. She was in the door looking at him when he raised his head. For one moment he stood still, staring, and then he started towards her with a quickened step. I started too, then, every step a torture, and as I limped ahead she made a gesture of terror and backed into the room before him. The door closed, and I listened for a pistol-shot and a scream. It must have been done with a knife, I thought, and quietly, for when I was within ten paces of the cabin he opened the door again. His face was very white; he held one hand behind him, and he was nervously fumbling at his chin with the other. As he stepped towards me I caught the handle of a pistol in my side pocket and waited. He looked at me sharply.

"Did you say the preacher lived up thar?" he asked.

"Yes," I said, breathlessly.

In the door-way just then stood the girl with a bonnet in her hand, and at a nod from him they started up the hill towards the cottage. They came down again after a while, he stalking ahead, and she, after the mountain fashion, behind. And after this fashion I saw them at sunset next day pass over the bridge and into the mouth of the Gap whence they came. Through this Gap come strange people and strange tales from the Kentucky hills. Over it, sometimes, is the span of a rainbow.

A TRICK O' TRADE

STRANGER, I'm a separate man, an' I don't inquizite into no man's business; but you ax me straight, an' I tell ye straight: You watch ole Tom!

Now, I'll take ole Tom Perkins' word agin anybody's 'ceptin' when hit comes to a hoss trade ur a piece o' land. Fer in the tricks o' sech, ole Tom 'lows—well, hit's diff'ent; an' I reckon, stranger, as how hit sorter is. He was a-stayin' at Tom's house, the furriner was, a-dickerin' fer a piece o' lan'—the same piece, mebbe, that you're atter now—an' Tom keeps him thar fer a week to beat him out'n a dollar, an' then won't let him pay nary a cent fer his boa'd. Now, stranger, that's Tom.

Well, Abe Shivers was a-workin' fer Tom— you've heerd tell o' Abe—an' the furriner wasn't more'n half gone afore Tom seed that Abe was up to some of his devilmint. Abe kin hatch up more devilmint in a minit than Satan hisself kin in a week; so Tom jes got Abe out'n the stable under a hoe-handle, an' tol' him to tell the whole thing straight ur he'd have to go to glory right thar. An' Abe tol'!

'Pears like Abe had foun' a streak o' iron ore on the lan', an' had racked his jinny right down to Hazlan an' tol' the furriner, who was thar a-buyin' wild lands right an' left. Co'se Abe was goin' to make the furriner whack up fer gittin' the lan' so cheap. Well, brother, the furriner come up to Tom's an' got Tom into one o' them new-fangled trades whut the furriners calls a option—t'other feller kin git out'n hit, but you can't. The furriner 'lowed he'd send his podner up thar next day to put the thing in writin' an' close up the trade. Hit looked like ole Tom was ketched fer shore, an' ef Tom didn't ra'r, I'd tell a man. He jes let that hoe-handle drap on Abe fer 'bout haffen hour, jes to give him time to study, an' next day thar was ole Tom a-settin' on his orchard fence a-lookin' mighty unknowin', when the furriner's podner come a-prancin' up an' axed ef old Tom Perkins lived thar.

Ole Tom jes whispers.

Now, I clean fergot to tell ye, stranger, that Abe Shivers nuver could talk out loud. He tol' so many lies that the Lawd—jes to make things even—sorter fixed Abe, I reckon, so he couldn't lie on more'n one side o' the river at a time. Ole Tom jes knowed t'other furriner had tol' this un 'bout Abe, an', shore 'nough, the feller says, sorter soft, says he:

" Aw, you air the feller whut foun' the ore? "

Ole Tom—makin' like he was Abe, mind ye
—jes whispers: " Thar hain't none thar."

Stranger, the feller mos' fell off'n his hoss.
" Whut? " says he. Ole Tom kep' a-whisper-
in': " Thar hain't no ore—no nothing; ole Tom
Perkins made me tell t'other furriner them lies."

Well, sir, the feller *was* mad. " Jes whut I
tol' that fool podner of mine," he says, an' he
pull out a dollar an' gives hit to Tom. Tom
jes sticks out his han' with his thum' turned in
jes so, an' the furriner says, " Well, ef you can't
talk, you kin make purty damn good signs ";
but he forks over four mo' dollars (he 'lowed
ole Tom had saved him a pile o' money), an'
turns his hoss an' pulls up agin. He was a-gittin'
the land so durned cheap that I reckon he jes
hated to let hit go, an' he says, says he: " Well,
hain't the groun' rich? Won't hit raise no to-
baccy nur corn nur nothin'? "

Ole Tom jes whispers:

" To tell you the p'int-blank truth, stranger,
that land's so durned pore that I hain't nuver
been able to raise my voice."

Now, brother, I'm a separ*ate* man, an' I don't
in*quiz*ite into no man's business—but you ax me
straight an' I tell ye straight. Ole Tom Perkins kin trade with furriners, fer he have l'arned
their ways. You watch ole Tom!

GRAYSON'S BABY

THE first snow sifted in through the Gap that night, and in a " shack " of one room and a low loft a man was dead, a woman was sick to death, and four children were barely alive; and nobody even knew. For they were hill people, who sicken, suffer, and sometimes die, like animals, and make no noise.

Grayson, the Virginian, coming down from the woods that morning, saw the big-hearted little doctor outside the door of the shack, walking up and down, with his hands in his pockets. He was whistling softly when Grayson got near, and, without stopping, pointed with his thumb within. The oldest boy sat stolidly on the one chair in the room, his little brother was on the floor hard by, and both were hugging a greasy stove. The little girl was with her mother in the bed, both almost out of sight under a heap of quilts. The baby was in a cradle, with its face uncovered, whether dead or asleep Grayson could not tell. A pine coffin was behind the door. It would not have been possible to add

to the disorder of the room, and the atmosphere
made Grayson gasp. He came out looking
white. The first man to arrive thereafter took
away the eldest boy, a woman picked the baby
girl from the bed, and a childless young couple
took up the pallid little fellow on the floor.
These were step-children. The baby boy that
was left was the woman's own. Nobody came
for that, and Grayson went in again and looked
at it a long while. So little, so old a human face
he had never seen. The brow was wrinkled as
with centuries of pain, and the little drawn
mouth looked as though the spirit within had
fought its inheritance without a murmur, and
would fight on that way to the end. It was the
pluck of the face that drew Grayson. " I'll take
it," he said. The doctor was not without his
sense of humor even then, but he nodded. " Cradle and all," he said, gravely. And Grayson put
both on one shoulder and walked away. He had
lost the power of giving further surprise in that
town, and had he met every man he knew, not
one of them would have felt at liberty to ask
him what he was doing. An hour later the
doctor found the child in Grayson's room, and
Grayson still looking at it.

" Is it going to live, doctor? "

The doctor shook his head. Doubtful.
Look at the color. It's starved. There's noth-

ing to do but to watch it and feed it. You can do that."

So Grayson watched it, with a fascination of which he was hardly conscious. Never for one instant did its look change—the quiet, unyielding endurance that no faith and no philosophy could ever bring to him. It was ideal courage, that look, to accept the inevitable but to fight it just that way. Half the little mountain town was talking next day—that such a tragedy was possible by the public road-side, with relief within sound of the baby's cry. The oldest boy was least starved. Might made right in an extremity like his, and the boy had taken care of himself. The young couple who had the second lad in charge said they had been wakened at daylight the next morning by some noise in the room. Looking up, they saw the little fellow at the fireplace breaking an egg. He had built a fire, had got eggs from the kitchen, and was cooking his breakfast. The little girl was mischievous and cheery in spite of her bad plight, and nobody knew of the baby except Grayson and the doctor. Grayson would let nobody else in. As soon as it was well enough to be peevish and to cry, he took it back to its mother, who was still abed. A long, dark mountaineer was there, of whom the woman seemed half-afraid. He followed Grayson outside.

"Say, podner," he said, with an unpleasant smile, "ye don't go up to Cracker's Neck fer nothin', do ye?"

The woman had lived at Cracker's Neck before she appeared at the Gap, and it did not come to Grayson what the man meant until he was half-way to his room. Then he flushed hot and wheeled back to the cabin, but the mountaineer was gone.

"Tell that fellow he had better keep out of my way," he said to the woman, who understood, and wanted to say something, but not knowing how, nodded simply. In a few days the other children went back to the cabin, and day and night Grayson went to see the child, until it was out of danger, and afterwards. It was not long before the women in town complained that the mother was ungrateful. When they sent things to eat to her the servant brought back word that she had called out, "'Set them over thar,' without so much as a thanky." One message was that "she didn' want no second-hand victuals from nobody's table." Somebody suggested sending the family to the poor-house. The mother said "she'd go out on her crutches and hoe corn fust, and that the people who talked 'bout sendin' her to the po'house had better save their breath to make prayers with." One day she was hired to do some washing. The

mistress of the house happened not to rise until ten o'clock. Next morning the mountain
woman did not appear until that hour. "She
wasn't goin' to work a lick while that woman
was a-layin' in bed," she said, frankly. And
when the lady went down town, she too disappeared. Nor would she, she explained to
Grayson, "while that woman was a-struttin'
the streets."

After that, one by one, they let her alone, and
the woman made not a word of complaint.
Within a week she was working in the fields,
when she should have been back in bed. The
result was that the child sickened again. The old
look came back to its face, and Grayson was
there night and day. He was having trouble out
in Kentucky about this time, and he went to the
Blue Grass pretty often. Always, however, he
left money with me to see that the child was
properly buried if it should die while he was
gone; and once he telegraphed to ask how it was.
He said he was sometimes afraid to open my
letters for fear that he should read that the baby
was dead. The child knew Grayson's voice, his
step. It would go to him from its own mother.
When it was sickest and lying torpid it would
move the instant he stepped into the room, and,
when he spoke, would hold out its thin arms,
without opening its eyes, and for hours Grayson

would walk the floor with the troubled little baby over his shoulder. I thought several times it would die when, on one trip, Grayson was away for two weeks. One midnight, indeed, I found the mother moaning, and three female harpies about the cradle. The baby was dying this time, and I ran back for a flask of whiskey. Ten minutes late with the whiskey that night would have been too late. The baby got to know me and my voice during that fortnight, but it was still in danger when Grayson got back, and we went to see it together. It was very weak, and we both leaned over the cradle, from either side, and I saw the pity and affection—yes, hungry, half-shamed affection—in Grayson's face. The child opened its eyes, looked from one to the other, and held out its arms to *me*. Grayson should have known that the child forgot—that it would forget its own mother. He turned sharply, and his face was a little pale. He gave something to the woman, and not till then did I notice that her soft black eyes never left him while he was in the cabin. The child got well; but Grayson never went to the shack again, and he said nothing when I came in one night and told him that some mountaineer—a long, dark fellow—had taken the woman, the children, and the household gods of the shack back into the mountains.

"They don't grieve long," I said, "these people."

But long afterwards I saw the woman again along the dusty road that leads into the Gap. She had heard over in the mountains that Grayson was dead, and had walked for two days to learn if it was true. I pointed back towards Bee Rock, and told her that he had fallen from a cliff back there. She did not move, nor did her look change. Moreover, she said nothing, and, being in a hurry, I had to ride on.

At the foot-bridge over Roaring Fork I looked back. The woman was still there, under the hot mid-day sun and in the dust of the road, motionless.

COURTIN' ON CUTSHIN

HIT was this way, stranger. When hit comes to handlin' a right peert gal, Jeb Somers air about the porest man on Fryin' Pan, I reckon; an' Polly Ann Sturgill have got the vineg'rest tongue on Cutshin or any other crick.

So the boys over on Fryin' Pan made it up to git 'em together. Abe Shivers—you've heerd tell o' Abe—tol' Jeb that Polly Ann had seed him in Hazlan (which she hadn't, of co'se), an' had said p'int-blank that he was the likeliest feller she'd seed in them mountains. An' he tol' Polly Ann that Jeb was ravin' crazy 'bout her. The pure misery of it jes made him plumb delirious, Abe said; an' 'f Polly Ann wanted to find her match fer languige an' talkin' out peert —well, she jes ought to strike Jeb Somers. Fact is, stranger, Jeb Somers air might' nigh a idgit; but Jeb 'lowed he'd rack right over on Cutshin an' set up with Polly Ann Sturgill; an' Abe tells Polly Ann the king bee air comin'. An' Polly Ann's cousin, Nance Osborn, comes over from Hell fer Sartain (whut runs into Kingdom-Come) to stay all night an' see the fun.

Now, I hain't been a-raftin' logs down to the settlemints o' Kaintuck fer nigh on to twenty year fer nothin'. An' I know gallivantin' is diff'ent with us mountain fellers an' you furriners, in the premises, anyways, as them lawyers up to court says; though I reckon hit's purty much the same atter the premises is over. Whar you says "courtin'," now, we says "talkin' to." Sallie Spurlock over on Fryin' Pan is a-talkin' to Jim Howard now. Sallie's sister hain't nuver talked to no man. An' whar you says "makin' a call on a young lady," we says "settin' up with a gal"! An', stranger, we does it. We hain't got more'n one room hardly ever in these mountains, an' we're jes obleeged to set up to do any courtin' at all.

Well, you go over to Sallie's to stay all night some time, an' purty soon atter supper Jim Howard comes in. The ole man an' the ole woman goes to bed, an' the chil'un an' you go to bed, an' ef you keeps one eye open you'll see Jim's cheer an' Sallie's cheer a-movin' purty soon, till they gets plumb together. Then, stranger, hit begins. Now I want ye to understand that settin' up means business. We don't 'low no foolishness in these mountains; an' 'f two fellers happens to meet at the same house, they jes makes the gal say which one she likes best, an' t'other one gits! Well, you'll see Jim put his arm 'round Sallie's neck an' whisper a long while—jes so. Mebbe you've noticed whut fellers us mountain folks air fer whisperin'. You've seed fellers a-whisperin' all over Hazlan on court day, hain't ye? Ole Tom Perkins 'll put his arm aroun' yo' neck an' whisper in yo' year ef he's ten miles out'n the woods. I reckon thar's jes so much devilmint a-goin' on in these mountains, folks is naturely afeerd to talk out loud.

Well, Jim lets go an' Sallie puts her arm aroun' Jim's neck an' whispers a long while—jes so; an' 'f you happen to wake up anywhar to two o'clock in the mornin' you'll see jes that a-goin' on. Brother, that's settin' up.

Well, Jeb Somers, as I was a-sayin' in the premises, 'lowed he'd rack right over on Cutshin an' set up with Polly Ann comin' Christmas night. An' Abe tells Polly Ann Jeb says he aims to have her fer a Christmas gift afore mornin'. Polly Ann jes sniffed sorter, but you know women folks air always mighty ambitious jes to *see* a feller anyways, 'f he's a-pinin' fer 'em. So Jeb come, an' Jeb was fixed up now fittin' to kill. Jeb had his hair oiled down nice an' slick, and his mustache was jes black as powder could make hit. Naturely hit was red; but a feller can't do nothin' in these mountains with a red mustache; an' Jeb had a big black ribbon tied in the butt o' the bigges' pistol Abe Shivers could borrer fer him—

118

hit was a badge o' death an' deestruction to his
enemies, Abe said, an' I tell ye Jeb did look like
a man. He never opened his mouth atter he
says "howdy" — Jeb never does say nothin';
Jeb's one o' them fellers whut hides thar lack o'
brains by a-lookin' solemn an' a-keepin' still, but
thar don't nobody say much tell the ole folks air
gone to bed, an' Polly Ann jes 'lowed Jeb was
a-waitin'. Fact is, stranger, Abe Shivers had got
Jeb a leetle disguised by liquer, an' he did look
fat an' sassy, ef he couldn't talk, a-settin' over
in the corner a-plunkin the banjer an' a-knockin'
off "Sour-wood Mountain" an' "Jinny Git
Aroun'" an' "Soapsuds over the Fence."

> "Chickens a-crowin' on Sour-wood Mountain,
>   Heh-o-dee-um-dee-eedy-dahdy-dee!
>   Git yo' dawgs an' we'll go huntin',
>   Heh-o-dee-um-dee-eedy-dahdy-dee!"

An' when Jeb comes to

> "I've got a gal at the head o' the holler,
>   Heh-o-dee-um-dee-eedy-dahdy-dee!"

he jes turns one eye 'round on Polly Ann, an'
then swings his chin aroun' as though he didn't
give a cuss fer nothin'.

> "She won't come, an' I won't foller,
>   Heh-o-dee-um-dee-eedy-dahdy-dee!"

Well, sir, Nance seed that Polly Ann was a-eyin' Jeb sort o' flustered like, an' she come might' nigh splittin' right thar an' a-sp'ilin' the fun, fer she knowed what a skeery fool Jeb was. An' when the ole folks goes to bed, Nance lays thar under a quilt a-watchin' an' a-listenin'. Well, Jeb knowed the premises, ef he couldn't talk, an' purty soon Nance heerd Jeb's cheer creak a leetle, an' she says, Jeb's a-comin', and Jeb was; an' Polly Ann 'lowed Jeb was jes a leetle *too* resolute an' quick-like, an' she got her hand ready to give him one lick anyways fer bein' so brigaty. I don't know as she'd 'a' hit him more'n *once*. Jeb had a farm, an' Polly Ann—well, Polly Ann was a-gittin' along. But Polly Ann sot thar jes as though she didn't know Jeb was a-comin', an' Jeb stopped once an' says,

" You hain't got nothin' agin me, has ye ? "

An' Polly Ann says, sorter quick,

" Naw; ef I had, I'd push it."

Well, Jeb mos' fell off his cheer, when, ef he hadn't been sech a skeery idgit, he'd 'a' knowed that Polly Ann was plain open an' shet a-biddin' fer him. But he sot thar like a knot on a log fer haffen hour, an' then he rickollected, I reckon, that Abe had tol' him Polly Ann was peppery an' he mustn't mind, fer Jeb begun a-movin' ag'in till he was slam-bang ag'in Polly Ann's cheer. An' thar he sot like a punkin, not sayin' a word nur doin' nothin'. An' while Polly Ann was a-wonderin' ef he was gone plumb crazy, blame me ef that durned fool didn't turn roun' to that peppery gal an' say,

"Booh, Polly Ann!"

Well, Nance had to stuff the bedquilt in her mouth right thar to keep from hollerin' out loud, fer Polly Ann's hand was a hangin' down by the cheer, jes a-waitin' fer a job, and Nance seed the fingers a-twitchin'. An' Jeb waits another haffen hour, an' Jeb says,

"Ortern't I be killed?"

"Whut fer?" says Polly Ann, sorter sharp. An' Jeb says, "Fer bein' so devilish."

Well, brother, Nance snorted right out thar, an' Polly Ann Sturgill's hand riz up jes once; an' I've heerd Jeb Somers say the next time he jumps out o' the Fryin' Pan he's a-goin' to take hell-fire 'stid o' Cutshin fer a place to light.

THE MESSAGE IN THE SAND

STRANGER, you furriners don't nuver seem to consider that a woman has always got the devil to fight in two people at once! Hit's two agin one, I tell ye, an' hit hain't fa'r.

That's what I said more'n two year ago, when Rosie Branham was a-layin' up thar at Dave Hall's, white an' mos' dead. An', *God,* boys, I says, that leetle thing in thar by her shorely can't be to blame.

Thar hain't been a word agin Rosie sence; an', stranger, I reckon thar nuver will be. Fer, while the gal hain't got hide o' kith or kin, thar air two fellers up hyeh sorter lookin' atter Rosie; an' one of 'em is the shootin'es' man on this crick, I reckon, 'cept one; an', stranger, that's t'other.

Rosie kep' her mouth shet fer a long while; an' I reckon as how the feller 'lowed she wasn't goin' to tell. Co'se the woman folks got hit out'n her — they al'ays gits whut they want, as you know—an' thar the sorry cuss was—a-livin' up thar in the Bend, jes aroun' that bluff o' lorrel yander, a-lookin' pious, an' a-singin', an' a-sayin' Amen louder 'n anybody when thar was meetin'.

122

Well, my boy Jim an' a lot o' fellers jes went up fer him right away. I don't know as the boys would 'a' killed him *exactly* ef they had kotched him, though they mought; but they got Abe Shivers, as tol' the feller they was a-comin'—you've heard tell o' Abe—an' they mos' beat Abraham Shivers to death. Stranger, the sorry cuss was Dave. Rosie hadn't no daddy an' no mammy; an' she was jes a-workin' at Dave's fer her victuals an' clo'es. 'Pears like the pore gal was jes tricked into evil. Looked like she was sorter 'witched — an' anyways, stranger, she was a-fightin' Satan in *herself*, as well as in Dave. Hit was two agin one, I tell ye, an' hit wasn't fa'r.

C'ose they turned Rosie right out in the road. I hain't got a word to say agin Dave's wife fer that; an' atter a while the boys lets Dave come back, to take keer o' his ole mammy, of co'se, but I tell ye Dave's a-playin' a purty lonsesome tune. He keeps purty shy *yit*. He don't nuver sa'nter down this way. 'Pears like he don't seem to think hit's healthy fer him down hyeh, an' I reckon Dave's right.

Rosie? Oh, well, I sorter tuk Rosie in myself. Yes, she's been livin' thar in the shack with me an' my boy Jim, an' the— Why, thar he is now, stranger. That's him a-wallerin' out thar in the road. Do you reckon thar'd be a single thing agin that leetle cuss ef he had to stan' up on Jedgment Day jes as he is now?

Look hyeh, stranger, whut you reckon the Lawd kep' a-writin' thar on the groun' that day when them fellers was a-pesterin' him about that pore woman? Don't you jes know he was a writin' 'bout sech as *him*—an' Rosie? I tell ye, brother, he writ thar jes what I'm al'ays a-sayin'.

Hit hain't the woman's fault. I said it more'n two years ago, when Rosie was up thar at ole Dave's, an' I said it yestiddy, when my boy Jim come to me an' 'lowed as how he aimed to take Rosie down to town to-day an' git married.

"You ricollect, dad," says Jim, "her mammy?"

"Yes, Jim," I says; "all the better reason not to be too hard on Rosie."

I'm a-lookin' fer 'em both back right now, stranger; an' ef you will, I'll be mighty glad to have ye stay right hyeh to the infair this very night. Thar nuver was a word agin Rosie afore, thar hain't been sence, an' you kin ride up an' down this river till the crack o' doom an' you'll nuver hear a word agin her ag'in. Fer, as I tol' you, my boy, Jim is the shootin'es' feller on this crick, I reckon, 'cept *one*, an', stranger, that's *me!*

124

THE SENATOR'S LAST TRADE

A DROVE of lean cattle were swinging
easily over Black Mountain, and behind
them came a big man with wild black hair and
a bushy beard. Now and then he would gnaw
at his mustache with his long, yellow teeth,
or would sit down to let his lean horse rest, and
would flip meaninglessly at the bushes with a
switch. Sometimes his bushy head would droop
over on his breast, and he would snap it up
sharply and start painfully on. Robber, cattle-
thief, outlaw he might have been in another century; for he filled the figure of any robber hero
in life or romance, and yet he was only the Senator from Bell, as he was known in the little
Kentucky capital; or, as he was known in his
mountain home, just the Senator, who had toiled
and schemed and grown rich and grown poor;
who had suffered long and was kind.

Only that Christmas he had gutted every
store in town. "Give me everything you have,
brother," he said, across each counter; and next
day every man, woman, and child in the mountain town had a present from the Senator's

hands. He looked like a brigand that day, as he looked now, but he called every man his brother, and his eye, while black and lustreless as night, was as brooding and just as kind.

When the boom went down, with it and with everybody else went the Senator. Slowly he got dusty, ragged, long of hair. He looked tortured and ever-restless. You never saw him still; always he swept by you, flapping his legs on his lean horse or his arms in his rickety buggy here, there, everywhere — turning, twisting, fighting his way back to freedom—and not a murmur. Still was every man his brother, and if some forgot his once open hand, he forgot it no more completely than did the Senator. He went very far to pay his debts. He felt honor bound, indeed, to ask his sister to give back the farm that he had given her, which, very properly people said, she declined to do. Nothing could kill hope in the Senator's breast; he would hand back the farm in another year, he said; but the sister was firm, and without a word still, the Senator went other ways and schemed through the nights, and worked and rode and walked and traded through the days, until now, when the light was beginning to glimmer, his end was come.

This was the Senator's last trade, and in

sight, down in a Kentucky valley, was home. Strangely enough, the Senator did not care at all, and he had just enough sanity left to wonder why, and to be worried. It was the "walking typhoid" that had caught up with him, and he was listless, and he made strange gestures and did foolish things as he stumbled down the mountain. He was going over a little knoll now, and he could see the creek that ran around his house, but he was not touched. He would just as soon have lain down right where he was, or have turned around and gone back, except that it was hot and he wanted to get to the water. He remembered that it was nigh Christmas; he saw the snow about him and the cakes of ice in the creek. He knew that he ought not to be hot, and yet he was—so hot that he refused to reason with himself even a minute, and hurried on. It was odd that it should be so, but just about that time, over in Virginia, a cattle-dealer, nearing home, stopped to tell a neighbor how he had tricked some black-whiskered fool up in the mountains. It may have been just when he was laughing aloud over there, that the Senator, over here, tore his woollen shirt from his great hairy chest and rushed into the icy stream, clapping his arms to his burning sides and shouting in his frenzy.

"If he had lived a little longer," said a constituent, " he would have lost the next election. He hadn't the money, you know."

" If he had lived a little longer," said the mountain preacher high up on Yellow Creek, " I'd have got that trade I had on hand with him through. Not that I wanted him to die, but if he had to—why——"

" If he had lived a little longer," said the Senator's lawyer, " he would have cleaned off the score against him."

" If he had lived a little longer," said the Senator's sister, not meaning to be unkind, " he would have got all I have."

That was what life held for the Senator. Death was more kind.

PREACHIN' ON KINGDOM-COME

I'VE told ye, stranger, that Hell fer Sartain empties, as it oughter, of co'se, into Kingdom-Come. You can ketch the devil 'most any day in the week on Hell fer Sartain, an' sometimes you can git Glory everlastin' on Kingdom-Come. Hit's the only meetin'-house thar in twenty miles aroun'.'

Well, the reg'lar rider, ole Jim Skaggs, was dead, an' the bretherin was a-lookin' aroun' fer somebody to step into ole Jim's shoes. Thar'd been one young feller up thar from the settlemints, a-cavortin' aroun', an' they was studyin' 'bout gittin' him.

"Bretherin' an' sisteren," I says, atter the leetle chap was gone, "he's got the fortitood to speak an' he shorely is well favored. He's got a mighty good hawk eye fer spyin' out evil—an' the gals; he can outholler ole Jim; an' if," I says, "any *idees* ever comes to him, he'll be a hell-rouser shore — but they ain't comin'!" An', so sayin', I takes my foot in my hand an' steps fer home.

Stranger, them fellers over thar hain't seed

much o' this world. Lots of 'em nuver seed the cyars; some of 'em nuver seed a wagon. An' atter jowerin' an' noratin' fer 'bout two hours, what you reckon they said they aimed to do? They believed they'd take that ar man Beecher, ef they could git him to come. They'd heerd o' Henry endurin' the war, an' they knowed he was agin the rebs, an' they wanted Henry if they could jes git him to come.

Well, I snorted, an' the feud broke out on Hell fer Sartain betwixt the Days an' the Dillons. Mace Day shot Daws Dillon's brother, as I rickollect — somep'n's al'ays a-startin' up that plaguey war an' a-makin' things frolicsome over thar — an' ef it hadn't a-been fer a tall young feller with black hair an' a scar across his forehead, who was a-goin' through the mountains a-settlin' these wars, blame me ef I believe thar ever would 'a' been any mo' preachin' on Kingdom-Come. This feller comes over from Hazlan an' says he aims to hold a meetin' on Kingdom-Come. "Brother," I says, "that's what no preacher have ever did whilst this war is a-goin' on." An' he says, sort o' quiet, "Well, then, I reckon I'll have to do what no preacher have ever did." An' I ups an' says: "Brother, an ole jedge come up here once from the settlemints to hold couht. 'Jedge,' I says, "that's what no jedge have ever did without soldiers since this war's been a-goin' on.' An', brother, the jedge's words was yours, p'int-blank. 'All right,' he says, 'then I'll have to do what no other jedge have ever did.' An', brother," says I to the preacher, "the jedge done it shore. He jes laid under the couht-house fer two days whilst the boys fit over him. An' when I sees the jedge a-makin' tracks fer the settlemints, I says, 'Jedge,' I says, 'you spoke a parable shore.'"

Well, sir, the long preacher looked jes as though he was a-sayin' to hisself, "Yes, I hear ye, but I don't heed ye," an' when he says, "Jes the same, I'm a-goin' to hold a meetin' on King-dom-Come," why, I jes takes my foot in my hand an' ag'in I steps fer home.

That night, stranger, I seed another feller from Hazlan, who was a-tellin' how this here preacher had stopped the war over thar, an' had got the Marcums an' Braytons to shakin' hands; an' next day ole Tom Perkins stops in an' says that *wharas* there mought 'a' been preachin' somewhar an' sometime, thar nuver had been *preachin'* afore on Kingdom-Come. So I goes over to the meetin'-house, an' they was all thar —Daws Dillon an' Mace Day, the leaders in the war, an' Abe Shivers (you've heerd tell o' Abe) who was a-carryin' tales from one side to t'other an' a-stirrin' up hell ginerally, as Abe most al'ays is; an' thar was Daws on one side o' the meetin'-house an' Mace on t'other, an' both jes a-watchin' fer t'other to make a move, an' thar'd 'a' been billy-hell to pay right thar! Stranger, that long preacher talked jes as easy as I'm a-talkin' now, an' hit was p'int-blank as the feller from Hazlan said. You jes ought 'a' heerd him tellin' about the Lawd a-bein' as pore as any feller thar, an' a-makin' barns an' fences an' ox-yokes an' sech like; an' not a-bein' able to write his own name—havin' to make his mark mebbe—when he started out to save the world. An' how they tuk him an' nailed him onto a cross when he'd come down fer nothin' but to save 'em; an' stuck a spear big as a corn-knife into his side, an' give him vinegar; an' his own mammy a-standin' down thar on the ground a-cryin' an' a-watchin' him; an' he a-fergivin' all of 'em then an' thar!

Thar nuver had been nothin' like that afore on Kingdom-Come, an' all along I heerd fellers a-layin' thar guns down; an' when the preacher called out fer sinners, blame me ef the fust feller that riz wasn't Mace Day. An' Mace says, " Stranger, 'f what you say is true, I reckon the Lawd 'll fergive me too, but I don't believe Daws Dillon ever will," an' Mace stood thar lookin' around fer Daws. An' all of a sudden the preacher got up straight an' called out, " Is thar a human in this house mean an' sorry enough to stand betwixt a man an' his Maker"? An' right thar, stranger, Daws riz. "Naw, by God, thar hain't!" Daws says, an' he walks up to Mace a-holdin' out his hand, an' they all busts out cryin' an' shakin' hands — Days an' Dillons—jes as the preacher had made 'em do over in Hazlan. An' atter the thing was over, I steps up to the preacher an' I says:

"Brother," I says, "*you* spoke a parable, shore."

THE PASSING OF ABRAHAM SHIVERS

I TELL ye, boys, hit hain't often a feller has the chance o' doin' so much good jes by *dyin'*. Fer 'f Abe Shivers air gone, shorely gone, the rest of us—every durn one of us—air a-goin' to be saved. Fer Abe Shivers—you hain't heerd tell o' *Abe?* Well, you must be a stranger in these mountains o' Kaintuck, shore.

"I don't know, stranger, as Abe ever was borned; nobody in these mountains knows it 'f he was. The fust time I ever heerd tell o' Abe he was a-hollerin' fer his rights one mawnin' at daylight, endurin' the war, jes outside o' ole Tom Perkins' door on Fryin' Pan. Abe was left thar by some home-gyard, I reckon. Well, nobody air ever turned out'n doors in these mountains, as you know, an' Abe got his rights that mawnin', an' he's been a-gittin' 'em ever sence. Tom already had a houseful, but 'f any feller got the bigges' hunk o' corn-bread, that feller was Abe; an' ef any feller got a-whalin', hit wasn't Abe.

"Abe tuk to lyin' right naturely—looked

like—afore he could talk. Fact is, Abe nuver
could do nothin' but jes whisper. Still, Abe
could manage to send a lie furder with that rat-
tlin' whisper than ole Tom could with that big
horn o' hisn what tells the boys the revenoos air
comin' up Fryin' Pan.

"Didn't take Abe long to git to braggin' an'
drinkin' an' naggin' an' hectorin'—everything,
'mos', 'cept fightin'. Nobody ever drawed Abe
Shivers into a fight. I don't know as he was
afeerd; looked like Abe was a-havin' sech a
tarnation good time with his devilmint he jes
didn't want to run no risk o' havin' hit stopped.
An' sech devilmint! Hit ud take a coon's age,
I reckon, to tell ye.

"The boys was a-goin' up the river one night
to git ole Dave Hall fer trickin' Rosie Branham
into evil. Some feller goes ahead an' tells ole
Dave they's a-comin'. Hit was Abe. Some
feller finds a streak o' ore on ole Tom Perkins'
land, an' racks his jinny down to town, an' tells
a furriner thar, an' Tom comes might' nigh
sellin' the land fer nothin'. Now Tom raised
Abe, but, jes the same, the feller was Abe.

"One night somebody guides the revenoos in
on Hell fer Sartain, an' they cuts up four stills.
Hit was Abe. The same night, mind ye, a feller
slips in among the revenoos while they's asleep,
and cuts off their hosses' manes an' tails—muled

every durned critter uv 'em. Stranger, hit was
Abe. An' as fer women-folks—well, Abe was
the ill-favoredest feller I ever see, an' he couldn't
talk; still, Abe was sassy, an' you know how
sass counts with the gals; an' Abe's whisperin'
come in jes as handy as any feller's settin' up;
so 'f ever you seed a man with a Winchester
a-lookin' fer the feller who had cut him out,
stranger, he was a-lookin' fer Abe.

"Somebody tells Harve Hall, up thar at a
dance on Hell fer Sartain one Christmas night,
that Rich Harp had said somep'n agin him an'
Nance Osborn. An' somebody tells Rich that
Harve had said somep'n agin Nance an' *him*.
Hit was one an' the same feller, stranger, an'
the feller was Abe. Well, while Rich an' Harve
was a-gittin' well, somebody runs off with Nance.
Hit was Abe. Then Rich an' Harve jes draws
straws fer a feller. Stranger, they drawed fer
Abe. Hit's purty hard to believe that Abe air
gone, 'cept that Rich Harp an' Harve Hall
don't never draw no straws fer nothin'; but 'f
by the grace o' Goddlemighty Abe air gone,
why, as I was a-sayin', the rest of us—every
durned one of us—air a-goin' to be saved, shore.
Fer Abe's gone fust, an' ef thar's only one Jedgment Day, the Lawd 'll nuver git to us."

A PURPLE RHODODENDRON

THE purple rhododendron is rare. Up in the Gap here, Bee Rock, hung out over Roaring Rock, blossoms with it—as a gray cloud purples with the sunrise. This rock was tossed lightly on edge when the earth was young, and stands vertical. To get the flowers you climb the mountain to one side, and, balancing on the rock's thin edge, slip down by roots and past rattlesnake dens till you hang out over the water and reach for them. To avoid snakes it is best to go when it is cool, at daybreak.

I know but one other place in this southwest corner of Virginia where there is another bush of purple rhododendron, and one bush only is there. This hangs at the throat of a peak not far away, whose ageless gray head is bent over a ravine that sinks like a spear thrust into the side of the mountain. Swept only by high wind and eagle wings as this is, I yet knew one man foolhardy enough to climb to it for a flower. He brought one blossom down: and to this day I do not know that it was not the act of a coward; yes, though Grayson did it, actually smiling all the way from peak to ravine, and though he was

my best friend—best loved then and since. I
believe he was the strangest man I have ever
known, and I say this with thought; for his ec-
centricities were sincere. In all he did I cannot
remember having even suspected anything the-
atrical but once.

We were all Virginians or Kentuckians at the
Gap, and Grayson was a Virginian. You might
have guessed that he was a Southerner from his
voice and from the way he spoke of women—
but no more. Otherwise, he might have been a
Moor, except for his color, which was about
the only racial characteristic he had. He had
been educated abroad and, after the English
habit, had travelled everywhere. And yet I can
imagine no more lonely way between the eterni-
ties than the path Grayson trod alone.

He came to the Gap in the early days, and just
why he came I never knew. He had studied the
iron question a long time, he told me, and what
I thought reckless speculation was, it seems, deliberate judgment to him. His money " in the
dirt," as the phrase was, Grayson got him a
horse and rode the hills and waited. He was
intimate with nobody. Occasionally he would
play poker with us and sometimes he drank a
good deal, but liquor never loosed his tongue.
At poker his face told as little as the back of his
cards, and he won more than admiration—even

from the Kentuckians, who are artists at the game; but the money went from a free hand, and, after a diversion like this, he was apt to be moody and to keep more to himself than ever. Every fortnight or two he would disappear, always over Sunday. In three or four days he would turn up again, black with brooding, and then he was the last man to leave the card-table or he kept away from it altogether. Where he went nobody knew; and he was not the man anybody would question.

One night two of us Kentuckians were sitting in the club, and from a home paper I read aloud the rumored engagement of a girl we both knew —who was famous for beauty in the Bluegrass, as was her mother before her and the mother before her—to an unnamed Virginian. Grayson sat near, smoking a pipe; and when I read the girl's name I saw him take the meerschaum from his lips, and I felt his eyes on me. It was a mystery how, but I knew at once that Grayson was the man. He sought me out after that and seemed to want to make friends. I was willing, or, rather he made me more than willing; for he was irresistible to me, as I imagine he would have been to anybody. We got to walking together and riding together at night, and we were soon rather intimate; but for a long time he never so much as spoke the girl's name. Indeed, he kept away from the Bluegrass for nearly two months; but when he did go he stayed a fort-night.

This time he came for me as soon as he got back to the Gap. It was just before midnight, and we went as usual back of Imboden Hill, through moon-dappled beeches, and Grayson turned off into the woods where there was no path, both of us silent. We rode through trem-ulous, shining leaves—Grayson's horse choosing a way for himself—and, threshing through a patch of high, strong weeds, we circled past an amphitheatre of deadened trees whose crooked arms were tossed out into the moonlight, and halted on the spur. The moon was poised over Morris's farm; South Fork was shining under us like a loop of gold, the mountains lay about in tranquil heaps, and the moon-mist rose luminous between them. There Grayson turned to me with an eager light in his eyes that I had never seen before.

" This has a new beauty to-night! " he said; and then "I told her about you, and she said that she used to know you—well." I was glad my face was in shadow—I could hardly keep back a brutal laugh—and Grayson, unseeing, went on to speak of her as I had never heard any man speak of any woman. In the end, he said that she had just promised to be his wife. I answered nothing. Other men, I knew, had said that with the same right, perhaps, and had gone from her to go back no more. And I was one of them. Grayson had met her at White Sulphur five years before, and had loved her ever since. She had known it from the first, he said, and I guessed then what was going to happen to him. I marvelled, listening to the man, for it was the star of constancy in her white soul that was most lustrous to him—and while I wondered the marvel became a commonplace. Did not every lover think his loved one exempt from the frailty that names other women? There is no ideal of faith or of purity that does not live in countless women to-day. I believe that; but could I not recall one friend who walked with Divinity through pine woods for one immortal spring, and who, being sick to death, was quite finished—learning her at last? Did I not know lovers who believed sacred to themselves, in the name of love, lips that had been given to many another without it? And now did I not know—but I knew too much, and to Grayson I said nothing.

That spring the "boom" came. Grayson's property quadrupled in value and quadrupled again. I was his lawyer, and I plead with him to sell; but Grayson laughed. He was not speculating; he had invested on judgment; he would sell only at a certain figure. The figure was actually reached, and Grayson let half go. The boom fell, and Grayson took the tumble with a jest. It would come again in the autumn, he said, and he went off to meet the girl at White Sulphur.

I worked right hard that summer, but I missed him, and I surely was glad when he came back. Something was wrong; I saw it at once. He did not mention her name, and for a while he avoided even me. I sought him then, and gradually I got him into our old habit of walking up into the Gap and of sitting out after supper on a big rock in the valley, listening to the run of the river and watching the afterglow over the Cumberland, the moon rise over Wallen's Ridge and the stars come out. Waiting for him to speak, I learned for the first time then another secret of his wretched melancholy. It was the hopelessness of that time perhaps, that disclosed it. Grayson had lost the faith of his childhood. Most men do that at some time or other, but Grayson had no business, no profession, no art in which to find relief. Indeed, there was but one substitute possible, and that came like a gift straight from the God whom he denied. Love came, and Grayson's ideals of love, as of everything else, were morbid and quixotic. He believed that he owed it to the woman he should marry never to have loved another. He had loved but one woman, he said, and he should love but one. I believed him then literally when he said that his love for the Kentucky girl was his religion now—the only anchor left him in his sea of troubles, the only star that gave him guiding light. Without this love, what then?

I had a strong impulse to ask him, but Grayson shivered, as though he divined my thought, and, in some relentless way, our talk drifted to the question of suicide. I was not surprised that he rather defended it. Neither of us said anything new, only I did not like the way he talked. He was too deliberate, too serious, as though he were really facing a possible fact. He had no religious scruples, he said, no family ties; he had nothing to do with bringing himself into life; why—if it was not worth living, not bearable— why should he not end it? He gave the usual authority, and I gave the usual answer. Religion aside, if we did not know that we were here for some purpose, we did not know that we were not; and here we were anyway, and our duty was plain. Desertion was the act of a coward, and that Grayson could not deny.

That autumn the crash of '91 came across the water from England, and Grayson gave up. He went to Richmond, and came back with money enough to pay off his notes, and I think it took nearly all he had. Still, he played poker steadily

now—for poker had been resumed when it was
no longer possible to gamble in lots—he drank
a good deal, and he began just at this time to
take a singular interest in our volunteer police
guard. He had always been on hand when there
was trouble, and I shan't soon forget him the
day Senator Mahone spoke, when we were
punching a crowd of mountaineers back with
cocked Winchesters. He had lost his hat in a
struggle with one giant; he looked half crazy
with anger, and yet he was white and perfectly
cool, and I noticed that he never had to tell a
man but once to stand back. Now he was the
first man to answer a police whistle. When we
were guarding Talt Hall, he always volunteered
when there was any unusual risk to run. When
we raided the Pound to capture a gang of desperadoes, he insisted on going ahead as spy; and
when we got restless lying out in the woods waiting for daybreak, and the captain suggested a
charge on the cabin, Grayson was by his side
when it was made. Grayson sprang through the
door first, and he was the man who thrust his
reckless head up into the loft and lighted a match
to see if the murderers were there. Most of us
did foolish things in those days under stress of
excitement, but Grayson, I saw, was weak enough
to be reckless. His trouble with the girl, whatever it was, was serious enough to make him ap-

parently care little whether he were alive or dead. And still I saw that not yet even had he lost hope. He was having a sore fight with his pride, and he got body-worn and heart-sick over it. Of course he was worsted, and in the end, from sheer weakness, he went back to her once more.

I shall never see another face like his when Grayson came back that last time. I never noticed before that there were silver hairs about his temples. He stayed in his room, and had his meals sent to him. He came out only to ride, and then at night. Waking the third morning at daybreak, I saw him through the window galloping past, and I knew he had spent the night on Black Mountain. I went to his room as soon as I got up, and Grayson was lying across his bed with his face down, his clothes on, and in his right hand was a revolver. I reeled into a chair before I had strength enough to bend over him, and when I did I found him asleep. I left him as he was, and I never let him know that I had been to his room; but I got him out on the rock again that night, and I turned our talk again to suicide. I said it was small, mean, cowardly, criminal, contemptible! I was savagely in earnest, and Grayson shivered and said not a word. I thought he was in better mind after that. We got to taking night rides again, and I stayed as closely to him as I could, for times got worse and trouble was upon everybody. Notes fell thicker than snowflakes, and, through the foolish policy of the company, foreclosures had to be made. Grayson went to the wall like the rest of us. I asked him what he had done with the money he had made. He had given away a great deal to poorer kindred; he had paid his dead father's debts; he had played away a good deal, and he had lost the rest. His faith was still imperturbable. He had a dozen rectangles of "dirt," and from these, he said, it would all come back some day. Still, he felt the sudden poverty keenly, but he faced it as he did any other physical fact in life—dauntless. He used to be fond of saying that no one thing could make him miserable. But he would talk with mocking earnestness about some much-dreaded combination; and a favorite phrase of his—which got to have peculiar significance—was "the cohorts of hell," who closed in on him when he was sick and weak, and who fell back when he got well. He had one strange habit, too, from which I got comfort. He would deliberately walk into and defy any temptation that beset him. That was the way he strengthened himself, he said. I knew what his temptation was now, and I thought of this habit when I found him asleep with his revolver, and I got hope from it now, when the dreaded combination (whatever that was) seemed actually to have come.

I could see now that he got worse daily. He stopped his mockeries, his occasional fits of reckless gayety. He stopped poker—resolutely— he couldn't afford to lose now; and, what puzzled me, he stopped drinking. The man simply looked tired, always hopelessly tired; and I could believe him sincere in all his foolish talk about his blessed Nirvana: which was the peace he craved, which was end enough for him.

Winter broke. May drew near; and one afternoon, when Grayson and I took our walk up through the Gap, he carried along a huge spyglass of mine, which had belonged to a famous old desperado, who watched his enemies with it from the mountain-tops. We both helped capture him, and I defended him. He was sentenced to hang—the glass was my fee. We sat down opposite Bee Rock, and for the first time Grayson told me of that last scene with her. He spoke without bitterness, and he told me what she said, word for word, without a breath of blame for her. I do not believe that he judged her at all; she did not know—he always said; she did not *know;* and then, when I opened my lips, Grayson reached silently for my wrist, and I can feel again the warning crush of his fingers, and I say nothing against her now.

I asked Grayson what his answer was.

"I asked her," he said, solemnly, "if she had even seen a purple rhododendron."

I almost laughed, picturing the scene—the girl bewildered by his absurd question—Grayson calm, superbly courteous. It was a mental peculiarity of his—this irrelevancy—and it was like him to end a matter of life and death in just that way.

"I told her I should send her one. I am waiting for them to come out," he added; and he lay back with his head against a stone and sighted the telescope on a dizzy point, about which buzzards were circling.

"There is just one bush of rhododendron up there," he went on. "I saw it looking down from the Point last spring. I imagine it must blossom earlier than that across there on Bee Rock, being always in the sun. No, it's not budding yet," he added, with his eye to the glass. "You see that ledge just to the left? I dropped a big rock from the Point square on a rattler who was sunning himself there last spring. I can see a foothold all the way up the cliff. It can be done," he concluded, in a tone that made me turn sharply upon him.

"Do you really mean to climb up there?" I asked, harshly.

"If it blossoms first up there—I'll get it where

148

it blooms first." In a moment I was angry and half sick with suspicion, for I knew his obstinacy; and then began what I am half ashamed to tell.

Every day thereafter Grayson took that glass with him, and I went along to humor him. I watched Bee Rock, and he that one bush at the throat of the peak—neither of us talking over the matter again. It was uncanny, that rivalry —sun and wind in one spot, sun and wind in another—Nature herself casting the fate of a half-crazed fool with a flower. It was utterly absurd, but I got nervous over it—apprehensive, dismal.

A week later it rained for two days, and the water was high. The next day the sun shone, and that afternoon Grayson smiled, looking through the glass, and handed it to me. I knew what I should see. One purple cluster, full blown, was shaking in the wind. Grayson was leaning back in a dream when I let the glass down. A cool breath from the woods behind us brought the odor of roots and of black earth; up in the leaves and sunlight somewhere a wood-thrush was singing, and I saw in Grayson's face what I had not seen for a long time, and that was peace—the peace of stubborn purpose. He did not come for me the next day, nor the next; but the next he did, earlier than usual.

" I am going to get that rhododendron," he said. " I have been half-way up—it can be reached." So had I been half-way up. With nerve and agility the flower could be got, and both these Grayson had. If he had wanted to climb up there and drop, he could have done it alone, and he would have known that I should have found him. Grayson was testing himself again, and, angry with him for the absurdity of the thing and with myself for humoring it, but still not sure of him, I picked up my hat and went. I swore to myself silently that it was the last time I should pay any heed to his whims. I believed this would be the last. The affair with the girl was over. The flower sent, I knew Grayson would never mention her name again.

Nature was radiant that afternoon. The mountains had the leafy luxuriance of June, and a rich, sunlit haze drowsed on them between the shadows starting out over the valley and the clouds so white that the blue of the sky looked dark. Two eagles shot across the mouth of the Gap as we neared it, and high beyond buzzards were sailing over Grayson's rhododendron.

I went up the ravine with him and I climbed up behind him—Grayson going very deliberately and whistling softly. He called down to me when he reached the shelf that looked half-way.

"You mustn't come any farther than this," he said. "Get out on that rock and I'll drop them down to you."

Then he jumped from the ledge and caught the body of a small tree close to the roots, and my heart sank at such recklessness and all my fears rose again. I scrambled hastily to the ledge, but I could get no farther. I might possibly make the jump he had made—but how should I ever get back? How would he? I called angrily after him now, and he wouldn't answer me. I called him a fool, a coward; I stamped the ledge like a child—but Grayson kept on, foot after hand, with stealthy caution, and the purple cluster nodding down at him made my head whirl. I had to lie down to keep from tumbling from the ledge; and there on my side, gripping a pine bush, I lay looking up at him. He was close to the flowers now, and just before he took the last upward step he turned and looked down that awful height with as calm a face as though he could have dropped and floated unhurt to the ravine beneath.

Then with his left hand he caught the ledge to the left, strained up, and, holding thus, reached out with his right. The hand closed about the cluster, and the twig was broken. Grayson gave a great shout then. He turned his head as though to drop them and, that far away, I heard the sibilant whir of rattles. I saw a snake's crest within a yard of his face, and, my God! I saw Grayson loose his left hand to guard it! The snake struck at his arm, and Grayson reeled and caught back once at the ledge with his left hand. He caught once, I say, to do him full justice; then, without a word, he dropped—and I swear there was a smile on his face when he shot down past me into the trees.

I found him down there in the ravine with nearly every bone in his body crushed. His left arm was under him, and outstretched in his right hand was the shattered cluster, with every blossom gone but one. One white half of his face was unmarked, and on it was still the shadow of a smile. I think it meant more than that Grayson believed that he was near peace at last. It meant that Fate had done the deed for him and that he was glad. Whether he would have done it himself, I do not know; and that is why I say that though Grayson brought the flower down— smiling from peak to ravine—I do not know that he was not, after all, a coward.

That night I wrote to the woman in Kentucky. I told her that Grayson had fallen from a cliff while climbing for flowers; and that he was dead. Along with these words, I sent a purple rhododendron.

MAN–HUNTING IN THE POUND

MAN-HUNTING IN THE POUND

THE pale lad from the Pound was telling news to an eager circle of men just outside the open window of the little mountain-hotel, and, inside, I dropped knife and fork to listen. The wily old " Daddy " of the Fleming boys had been captured; the sons were being hemmed in that very day, and a fight between sheriff's posse and outlaws was likely any hour.

Ten minutes later I was astride a gray mule, and with an absurd little .32 Smith & Wesson popgun on my hip—the only weapon I could find in town—was on my way to the Pound.

Our volunteer police-guard down at " The Gap," twenty miles away, was very anxious to capture those Fleming boys. Talton Hall, feud-leader and desperado, had already been hanged, and so had his bitter enemy, the Red Fox of the Mountains. With the Fleming outlaws brought to justice, the fight of the guard for law and order was about won. And so, as I was a member of that guard, it behooved me to hurry— which I did.

The Gap is in the southwestern corner of old Virginia, and is a ragged gash down through the Cumberland Mountains to the water level of a swift stream that there runs through a mountain of limestone and between beds of iron ore and beds of coking coal. That is why some three-score young fellows gathered there from Blue-grass Kentucky and Tide-water Virginia not many years ago, to dig their fortunes out of the earth. Nearly all were college graduates, and all were high-spirited, adventurous and well-born. They proposed to build a town and, incidentally, to make cheaper and better iron there than was made anywhere else on the discovered earth.

A " boom " came. The labor and capital question was solved instantly, for every man in town was straightway a capitalist. You couldn't get a door hung—every carpenter was a meteoric Napoleon of finance. Every young blood in town rode Blue-grass saddle-horses and ate eight-o'clock dinners—making many dollars each day and having high jinks o' nights at the club, which, if you please, entertained, besides others of distinction, a duke and duchess who had warily eluded the hospitality of New York. The woods were full of aristocrats and plutocrats—American and English. The world itself seemed to be moving that way, and the Gap stretched its jaws wide with a grin of welcome. Later, you could get a door hung, but here I draw the veil. It was magnificent, but it was not business.

At the high tide, even, the Gap was, however, something of a hell-hole for several reasons; and the clash of contrasts was striking. The Kentucky feudsmen would chase each other there, now and then, from over Black Mountain; and the toughs on the Virginia side would meet there on Saturdays to settle little differences of opinion and sentiment. They would quite take the town sometimes—riding through the streets, yelling and punctuating the sign of our one hotel with pistol-bullet periods to this refrain:

. . . . G.r.a.n.d C.e.n.t.r.a.l H.o.t.e.l. . . . .

Hell!   Hell!   Hell!

—keeping time meanwhile, like darkies in a hoe-down. Or, a single horseman might gallop down one of our wooden sidewalks, with his reins between his teeth, and firing into the ground with a revolver in each hand. All that, too, was magnificent, but it was not business. The people who kept store would have to close up and take to the woods.

And thus arose a unique organization—a volunteer police-guard of gentlemen, who carried pistol, billy, and whistle, and did a policeman's work—hewing always strictly to the line of the law.

The result was rather extraordinary. The Gap soon became the only place south of Mason and Dixon's line, perhaps, where a street fight of five minutes' duration, or a lynching, was impossible. A yell, a pistol-shot, or the sight of a drunken man, became a rare occurrence. Local lawlessness thus subdued, the guard extended its benign influence—creating in time a public sentiment fearless enough to convict a desperado, named Talt Hall; and, guarding him from rescue by his Kentucky clansmen for one month at the county-seat, thus made possible the first hanging that mountain-region had ever known.

After that the natives, the easy-going, tolerant good people, caught the fever for law and order, for, like lawlessness, law, too, is contagious. It was they who guarded the Red Fox, Hall's enemy, to the scaffold, and it was they who had now taken up our hunt for the Red Fox's accomplices—the Fleming outlaws of the Pound.

We were anxious to get those boys—they had evaded and mocked us so long. Usually they lived in a cave, but lately they had grown quite "tame." From working in the fields, dressed in women's clothes, they got to staying openly at home and lounging around a cross-roads store at the Pound. They even had the impudence to vote for a sheriff and a county judge. They levied on their neighbors for food and clothes, and so bullied and terrorized the Pound that nobody dared to deny them whatever they asked, or dared to attempt an arrest. At last, they got three or four recruits, and tying red strips of flannel to their shoulders and Winchesters, drilled in the county road, mocking our drill at the county-seat when we were guarding Talton Hall.

This taunt was a little too much, and so we climbed on horseback late one afternoon, wrapped our guns in overcoats, and started out for an all-night ride, only to be turned back again at the foot of Black Mountain by our captain and first lieutenant, who had gone over ahead of us as spies. The outlaws were fighting among themselves; one man was killed, and we must wait until they got " tame " again.

A few weeks later the guard rode over again, dashed into the Fleming cabin at daybreak and captured a houseful of screaming women and children—to the great disgust of the guard and to the great humor of the mountaineers, who had heard of our coming and gone off, dancing, down the road only an hour before. It was then that the natives, emulating our example, took up the search. They were doing the work now, and it was my great luck to be the only member of the guard who knew what was going on.

The day was hot the road dusty, and the gray mule was slow. Within two hours I was at the head of the Pound—a wild, beautiful, lawless region that harbored the desperadoes of Virginia and Kentucky, who could do mischief in either State and step to refuge across the line. Far ahead, I could see a green dip in the mountains where the Red Fox and the Fleming boys had shot the Mullins family of moonshiners to death from ambush one sunny morning in May.

Below, sparkled Pound River roaring over a milldam, and by the roadside, as I went down, I found the old miller alone. The posse of natives had run upon the Flemings that morning, he said, and the outlaws, after a sharp fight, had escaped —wounded. The sheriff was in charge of the searching party, and he believed that the Flemings would be caught now, for sure.

"Which way?" I asked.

The old fellow pointed down a twisting, sunlit ravine, dense with woods, and I rode down the dim creek that twisted through it. Half an hour later I struck a double log-cabin with quilts hanging in its windows—which was unusual. An old woman appeared in the doorway—a tall, majestic old tigress, with head thrown back and a throat so big that it looked as though she had a goitre.

"Who lives here?"

"The Flemingses lives hyeh," she said, quietly.

I was startled. I had struck the outlaws' cabin by chance, and so, to see what I might learn, I swung from the gray mule and asked for a glass of buttermilk. A handsome girl of twenty, a Fleming sister, with her dress open at the throat, stepped from the door and started to the spring-house. Through the door I could see another woman—wife of one of the outlaws—ill. A "base-born" child toddled toward me, and a ten-year-old boy—a Fleming brother—with keen eyes and a sullen face, lay down near me—watching me, like a snake in the grass.

The old woman brought out a chair and lighted a pipe.

"Whar air ye from, and what mought yo' name be?"

I evaded half the inquiry.

"I come from the Blue-grass, but I'm living at the Gap just now." She looked at me keenly, as did the snake in the grass, and I turned my chair so that I could watch that boy.

"Was you over hyeh that night when them fellows from the Gap run in on us?"

"No."

The old woman's big throat shook with quiet laughter. The girl laughed and the woman through the door laughed in her apron, but the boy's face moved not a muscle. It was plain that we had no monopoly of the humor of that daybreak dash into a house full of women and children.

"One fool feller stuck his head up into the loft and lit a match to see if my boys was up thar. *Lit* a *match!* He wouldn't 'a' had no head ef they had been." She laughed again, and drew on her pipe.

"I give 'em coffee," she went on, "while they waited for my boys to come back, an' all I axed 'em was not to hurt 'em if they could help it." Then she broached the point at issue herself.

"I s'pose you've heerd about the fight this mornin'?"

"Yes."

"I reckon you know my boys is hurt—mebbe they're dead in the woods somewhar now." She spoke with little sadness and with no animus whatever. There was no use trying to conceal my purpose down there—I saw that at once— and I got up to leave. She would not let me pay for the buttermilk.

"Ef you git hold of 'em—I wish you wouldn't harm 'em," she said, as I climbed on the gray mule, and I promised her that if they were caught unharmed, no further harm should come to them; and I rode away, the group sitting motionless and watching me.

For two hours I ambled along the top of a spur, on a pretty shaded road with precipitous woods on each side, and now and then an occasional cabin, but not a human being was in sight —not for long. Sometimes I would see a figure flitting around a corner of a cabin; sometimes a door would open a few inches and close quickly; and I knew the whole region was terrorized. For two hours I rode on through the sunlight and beauty of those lonely hills, and then I came on a crowd of mountaineers all armed with Winchesters, and just emerging from a cabin by the roadside. It was one division of the searching party, and I joined them. They were much amused when they saw the Christmas toy with which I was armed.

" S'pose one o' the Flemings had stepped out'n the bushes an' axed ye what ye was doin' down hyeh—what would ye 'a' said? "

That might have been embarrassing, and I had to laugh. I really had not thought of that.

One man showed me the Winchester they had captured—Heenan's gun. Tied to the meat-house and leaping against a rope-tether was a dog—which, too, they had captured—Heenan's dog. As we started out the yard " Gooseneck "

John Branham, with a look of disgust at my pistol, whipped out one of his own—some two feet long—for me to swing on my other hip. Another fellow critically took in my broad-brim straw hat.

"Hell!" he said. "That won't do. They can see that a mile through the woods. I'll get ye a hat." And he went back into the cabin and brought out a faded slouch-hat.

"That's Heenan's!" he said. That, too, they had captured.

And so I wore Heenan's hat—looking for Heenan.

Half a mile down the road we stepped aside twenty yards into the bushes. There was the cave in which the outlaws had lived. There were in it several blankets, a little bag of meal, and some bits of ham. Right by the side of the road was a huge pile of shavings, where the two outlaws had whittled away many a sunny hour. Half an hour on, down a deep ravine and up a long slope, and we were on a woody knoll where the fight had taken place that morning. The little trees looked as though a Gatling gun had been turned loose on them.

The posse had found out where the Flemings were, the night before, by capturing the old Fleming mother while she was carrying them a bag of provisions. As they lay in the brush, she had come along, tossing stones into the bushes to attract the attention of her sons. One of the men had clicked the slide of his Winchester, and the poor old woman, thinking that was the signal from one of her boys, walked toward them, and they caught her and kept her prisoner all night in the woods. Under her apron, they found the little fellow who had lain like a snake in the grass beside me back at the cabin, and, during the night, he had slipped away and escaped and gone back to the county-seat, twenty miles away, on foot, to tell his father, who was a prisoner there, what was taking place at home.

At daybreak, when the posse was closing in on the Flemings, the old woman sprang suddenly to her feet and shouted shrilly: " Run down the holler, boys; run down the holler ! "

The ways of rude men, naturally, are not gentle, and the sheriff sprang out and caught the old woman by the throat and choked her cries; and they led her to the rear—weeping and wringing her hands.

A few minutes later, as the men slipped forward through the woods and mist, they came upon the Flemings crouched in the bushes, and each creeping for a tree. " Gooseneck " John Branham—so called because of the length of his neck—Doc Swindall and Ed Hall opened fire.

For twenty minutes those two Fleming boys fought twenty-two men fiercely.

"Just looked like one steady flame was a-comin' out o' each man's Winchester all the time," said Branham, pointing to two bullet-pecked trees behind which the outlaws had stood. "I was behind this birch," laying his hand on a tree as big as his thigh, and pointing out where the Flemings had drilled three bullet-holes in it between his neck and his waistband.

"I seed Jim Hale pokin' his gun around this hyeh tree and pumpin' it off inter the ground," said Hall, "an' I couldn't shoot for laughin'."

"Well," said Swindall, "I was tryin' to git in a shot from the oak there, and something struck me and knocked me out in the bushes. I looked around, and damn me if there wasn't seven full-grown men behind my tree."

It had evidently been quite warm for a while, until Branham caught Heenan in the shoulder with a load of buckshot. Heenan's hat went off, his gun dropped to his feet; he cried simply:

"Oh——you!" Then he ran.

Cal Fleming, too, ran then, and the posse fired after them. The dog, curiously enough, lay where he had lain during the fight, at the base of Heenan's tree—and so hat, dog, and gun were captured. I had wondered why the posse had not pursued the Flemings after wounding them, and I began to understand. They were so elated at having been in a fight and come out safe, that they stopped to cook breakfast, gather mementos, and talk it all over.

Ten minutes later we were at the cabin, where the fugitives had stopped to get some coffee.

"They was pretty badly hurt, I reckon," said the woman who had given them something to eat.

"Heenan's shoulder was all shot up, an' I reckon I could git my hand into a hole in Cal's back. Cal was groanin' a good deal, an' had to lay down every ten yards."

We went on hurriedly, and in an hour we struck the main body of the searching party, and as soon as the sheriff saw me, he came running forward. Now, the guard at the Gap had such a reputation that any member of it was supposed to be past-master in the conduct of such matters as were now pending. He immediately called me "Captain," and asked me to take charge of the party. I looked round at them, and I politely veered from the honor. Such a tough-looking gang it has rarely been my good luck to see, and I had little doubt that many of them were worse than the Fleming boys. One tall fellow particularly attracted my attention; he was fully six and one-half feet high; he was very slender, and his legs and arms were the longest I have ever seen swung to a human frame. He had sandy hair, red eyes, high cheek-bones, and on each cheek was a diminutive boil. About his waist was strapped a huge revolver, and to the butt of this pistol was tied a big black bow-ribbon—tied there, no doubt, by his sweetheart, as a badge of death or destruction to his enemies. He looked me over calmly.

" Hev you ever searched for a dead man? " he asked deeply.

It was humiliating to have to confess it in that crowd, but I had not—not then.

" Well, I hev," he said, significantly.

I had little doubt, and for one, perhaps, of his own killing.

In the hollow just below us was the cabin of Parson Swindall—a friend of the Flemings. The parson thought the outlaws dying or dead, and he knew the cave to which they must have dragged themselves to die. If I got permission from the old Fleming mother, he would guide me, he said, to the spot. I sent back a messenger, promising that the bodies of her sons should not be touched, if they were dead, nor should they be further harmed if they were still alive. The fierce old woman's answer came back in an hour.

" She'd ruther they rotted out in the woods."

"Hev you ever searched for a dead man?"

Next morning I stretched the men out in a long line, thirty feet apart, and we started on the search. I had taken one man and spent the night in the parson's cabin hoping that, if only wounded, the Flemings might slip in for something to eat; but I had a sleepless, useless night. Indeed, the search had only a mild interest and no excitement. We climbed densely thicketed hills, searched ravines, rocks, caves, swam the river backward and forward, tracking suspicious footsteps in the mud and through the woods. I had often read of pioneer woodcraft, and I learned, during these three days, that the marvellous skill of it still survives in the Southern mountains.

It was dangerous work; dangerous for the man who should run upon the outlaws, since these would be lying still to hear anyone approach them, and would thus " have the drop " from ambush. Once, to be sure, we came near a tragedy. At one parting of two roads several of us stopped to decide which road we should take. At that moment the Fleming boys were lying in the bushes twenty yards away, with their Winchesters cocked and levelled at us over a log, and only waiting for us to turn up that path to open fire. As I was told afterward, Heenan, very naturally, had his Winchester pointed on his hat, which, at that moment, was on my head.

By a lucky chance I decided to take the other path. Otherwise, I should hardly be writing these lines to-day.

For three days we searched, only to learn, or rather to be told, which was not the truth, that, in women's dress, the Flemings had escaped over into Kentucky. As a matter of fact, they lay two weeks in a cave, Cal flat on his back and letting the water from the roof of the cave drip, hour by hour, on a frightful wound in his breast.

For several months they went uncaptured, until finally three of the men who were with me, " Gooseneck " John Branham, Ed Hall, and Doc Swindall, located them over the border in West Virginia. Of course a big reward was offered for each, or they were " rewarded," as the mountaineers say. The three men closed in on them in a little store one morning. Cal Fleming was reading a letter when the three surged in at the door, and Hall, catching Cal by the lapel of his coat, said quietly :

" You are my prisoner."

Cal sprang back to break the hold, and Hall shot him through the breast, killing him outright. Heenan, who was not thought to be dangerous, sprang at the same instant ten feet away, and his first shot caught Hall in the back of the head, dropping the officer to his knees. Thinking he had done for Hall, Heenan turned on Branham and Swindall, and shot Branham through both lungs and Swindall through the neck—dropping both to the floor. This left the duel between Hall on his knees and Heenan. At last a lucky shot from Hall's pistol struck Heenan's pistol hand, lacerating the fingers and making him drop his weapon. Heenan ran into the back room then, and, finding no egress, reappeared in the doorway, with his bloody hands above his head.

"Well, Ed," he said, simply, "I can't do no more."

Six months later Heenan Fleming was brought back to the county-seat to be tried for his life, and I felt sure that he would meet his end on the scaffold where Talton Hall and Red Fox had suffered death.

As he sat there in the prisoner's box, his face pale and flecked with powder, I could see a sunken spot in his jaw, through which one of Hall's bullets had gone, and his bright, black eyes gleamed fire. I stepped up to him. I thought there was no chance of his escaping the gallows; but, if he did escape, I wanted to be as friendly with him as possible.

"Heenan," I said, "did you ever get your hat back?"

" No," he said.

" Well, if you come clear, go up to the store and get the best hat in the house, and have it charged to me."

Heenan smiled.

Now, by a curious chance, the woman on whose testimony the Red Fox had been hanged, had died meanwhile. Some people said she had been purposely put out of the way to avoid further testimony. At any rate, through her death, Heenan did come clear, and the last time I saw him, he was riding out of the town on a mule, with his baby in front of him and on his head a brand-new derby hat—mine.

DOWN THE KENTUCKY ON A RAFT

DOWN THE KENTUCKY ON
A RAFT

THE heart of the Blue-grass in the middle of a sunny afternoon. An hour thence, through a rolling sweep of greening earth and woodland, through the low, poor hills of the brush country and into the oasis of Indian Old Fields, rich in level meadow-lands and wheat-fields. In the good old days of the war-whoop and the scalping-knife, the savage had there one of the only two villages that he ever planted in the "Dark and Bloody Ground." There Daniel Boone camped one night and a pioneer read him "Gulliver's Travels," and the great Daniel called the little stream at their feet Lulli-bigrub—which name it bears to-day. Another hour between cliffs and pointed peaks and cas-tled rocky summits, and through laurel and rho-dodendron to the Three Forks of the Kentucky. Up the Middle Fork then and at dusk the end of the railroad in the heart of the mountains and Jackson—the county-seat of "Bloody Breath-itt"—once the seat of a lively feud and still the possible seat of another, in spite of the fact that with a manual training-school and a branch of a Blue-grass college, it is also the seat of learning and culture for the region drained by Cutshin, Hell-fer-Sartain, Kingdom Come, and other little streams of a nomenclature not less picturesque. Even Hell-fer-Sartain is looking up. A pious lady has established a Sunday-school on Hell-fer-Sartain. A humorous bookseller has offered to give it a library on the condition that he be allowed to design a book-plate for the volumes. And the Sunday-school is officially known as the " Hell-fer-Sartain Sunday-school." From all these small tributaries of the Kentucky, the mountaineer floats logs down the river to the capital in the Blue-grass. Not many years ago that was his chief reason and his only one for going to the Blue-grass, and down the Kentucky on a raft was the best way for him to get there. He got back on foot. But, coming or going, by steam, water, horseback, or afoot, the trip is well worth while.

At Jackson a man with a lantern put me in a " hack," drove me aboard a flat boat, ferried me over with a rope cable, cracked his whip, and we went up a steep, muddy bank into the town. All through the Cumberland valleys, nowadays, little " boom " towns with electric lights, waterworks, and a street-railway make one think of the man who said " give him the luxuries of life and he would do without the necessaries." I did not know that Jackson had ever had a boom, but I thought so when I saw between the flapping curtains of the " hack " what seemed to be a white sidewalk of solid cement.

" Hello," I said, " is that a sidewalk? " The driver grunted, quickly :

" Hit's the side you walk on! "

A wheel of the hack went down to the hub in mud just then and I felt the force of his humor better next morning—I was to get such humor in plenty on the trip—when I went back to the river that same way. It was not a sidewalk of cement but a whitewashed board fence that had looked level in the dark, and except along a muddy foot-wide path close to the fence, passing there, for anything short of a stork on stilts, looked dangerous. I have known mules to drown in a mountain mud-hole.

The " tide," as the mountaineer calls a flood, had come the day before and, as I feared, the rafts were gone. Many of them had passed in the night, and there was nothing to do but to give chase. So I got a row-boat and a mountaineer, and, taking turns at the oars, we sped down the swift yellow water at the clipping rate of ten miles an hour.

As early as the late days of August the mountaineer goes " logging " in order to cut the trees before the sap rises, so that the logs can dry better all winter and float better in the spring. Before frost comes, on river-bank, hill-side, and mountain-top, the cool morning air is resonant with the ring of axes, the singing whistle of big saws, the crash of giant poplar and oak and chestnut down through the lesser growth under them, and the low boom that echoes through the woods when the big trees strike the earth. All winter this goes on. With the hammer of the woodpecker in the early spring, you hear the cries of ox-drivers "snaking" the logs down the mountain-side to the edge of some steep cliff, where they are tumbled pell-mell straight down to the bank of the river, or the bank of some little creek that runs into it. It takes eight yoke of oxen, sometimes, to drag the heart of a monarch to the chute, and there the logs are "rafted"— as the mountaineer calls the work; that is, they are rolled with hand-spikes into the water and lashed side by side with split saplings—lengthwise in the broad Big Sandy, broadside in the narrow Kentucky. Every third or fourth log is a poplar, because that wood is buoyant and will help float the chestnut and the oak. At bow and stern, a huge long limber oar is rigged on a turning stile, the raft is anchored to a tree with a cable of rope or grapevine, and there is a patient wait for a "tide." Some day in March or April—sometimes not until May—mist and clouds loose the rain in torrents, the neighbors gather, the cable is slipped, and the raft swings out the mouth of the creek on its long way to the land of which, to this day, the average mountaineer knows hardly less than that land knows of him.

Steadily that morning we kept the clumsy row-boat sweeping around green-buttressed points and long bends of the river, between high vertical cliffs overspread with vines and streaked white with waterfalls, through boiling eddies and long, swift, waving riffles, in an exhilaration that seems to come to running blood and straining muscles only in lonely wilds. Once a boy shied a stone down at us from the point of a cliff hundreds of feet sheer overhead.

" I wish I had my 44," said the mountaineer, looking wistfully upward.

" You wouldn't shoot at him? "

" I'd skeer him a leetle, I reckon," he said, dryly, and then he told me stories of older and fiercer days when each man carried a " gun," and often had to use it to secure a landing on dark nights when the loggers had to tie up to the bank. When the moon shines, the rafts keep going night and day.

" When the river's purty swift, you know, it's hard to stop a raft. I've seen a raft slash down

179

through the bushes for two miles before a fellow could git a rope around a tree. So sometimes we had to ketch hold of another feller's raft that was already tied up, and, as there was danger o' pullin' his loose, the feller'd try to keep us off. That's whar the 44's come in. And they do it yit," he said, as, later, I learned for myself.

Here and there were logs and splintered saplings thrown out on the bank of the river—signs of wreckage where a raft had " bowed "; that is, the bow had struck the bank at the bend of the river, the stern had swung around to the other shore, and the raft had hunched up in the middle like a bucking horse. Standing upright, the mountaineer can ride a single log down a swift stream, even when his weight sinks it a foot or two under the surface, but he finds it hard and dangerous to stay aboard a raft when it " bows."

" I was bringin' a raft out o' Leatherwood Creek below heah "—only that was not the name he gave the creek—" and we bowed just before we got to the river. Thar was a kind of a idgit on board who was just a-ridin' down the creek fer fun, and when I was throwed out in the woods I seed him go up in the air and come down kerflop in the water. He went under the raft, and crawled out about two hundred yards down the river. We axed him to git on agin, but that idgit showed more sense than I knowed he had. He said he'd heerd o' hell and high water, and he'd been under one and mighty close to t'other, and he reckoned he'd stay whar he was."

It was getting toward noon now. We had made full forty miles, and Leatherwood was the next stream below.

"We mought ketch a raft thar," said the mountaineer; and we did. Sweeping around the bend I saw a raft two hundred feet long at the mouth of the creek—tugging at its anchor—and a young giant of a mountaineer pushing the bow-oar to and fro through the water to test its suppleness. He had a smile of pure delight on his bearded, winning face when we shot the row-boat alongside.

"I tell you, Jim," he said, "hit's a sweet-pullin' oar."

"It shorely is, Tom," said Jim. "Heah's a furriner that wants to go down the river with ye."

"All right," said the giant, hospitably. "We're goin' just as soon as we can git off."

On the bank was a group of men, women, and children gathered to watch the departure. In a basin of the creek above, men up to their waists in water were "rafting" logs. Higher above was a chute, and down it rolled more logs, jumping from end to end, like jackstraws. Higher, I could hear the hammer of a wood-pecker;

higher still, the fluting of a wood-thrush, and still higher, an ox-driver's sharp cry. The vivid hues of dress and shawl on the bank seemed to strike out sharply every color-note in the green wall behind them, straight up to the mountain-top. It was as primitive and simple as Arcady.

Down the bank came old Ben Sanders, as I learned later, shouting his good-bys, without looking behind him as he slipped down the bank. Close after him, his son, young Ben, with a huge pone of corn-bread three feet square. The boy was so trembling with excitement over his first trip that he came near dropping it. Then a mountaineer with lank, long hair, the scholar of the party, and Tim, guilty of humor but once on the trip — solemn Tim. Two others jumped aboard with bacon and coffee—passengers like myself. Tom stood on shore with one hand on the cable, while he said something now and then to a girl in crimson homespun who stood near, looking downward. Now and then one of the other women would look at the two and laugh.

" All right now, Tom," shouted old Ben, " let her loose ! "

Tom thrust out his hand, which the girl took shyly.

" Don't fergit, Tom," she said. Tom laughed —there was little danger that Tom would forget

—and with one twist of his sinewy hands he threw the loop of the grapevine clear of the tree and, for all his great bulk, sprang like a cat aboard the raft, which shot forward with such lightness that I was nearly thrown from my feet.

"Good-by, Ben!"

"Good-by, Molly!"

"So long, boys!"

"Don't you fergit that caliker, now, Ben."

"I won't."

"Tom," called a mountaineer, "ef you git drunk an' spend yo' money, Nance heah says she won't marry ye when you come back." Nance slapped at the fellow, and the giant smiled. Then one piping voice:

"Don't fergit my terbacky, Ben."

"All right, Granny—I won't," answered old Ben, and, as we neared the bend of the river, he cried back:

"Take that saddle home I borrowed o' Joe Thomas, an' don't fergit to send that side of bacon to Mandy Longnecker, an'—an'—" and then I got a last glimpse of the women shading their patient eyes to watch the lessening figures on the raft and the creaking oars flashing white in the sunlight; and I thought of them going back to their lonely little cabins on this creek to await the home-coming of the men. If the mountain-women have any curiosity about that distant land, the Blue-grass "settlemints," they never show it. I have never known a mountain-woman to go down the river on a raft. Perhaps they don't care to go; perhaps it is not proper, for their ideas of propriety are very strict; perhaps the long trip back on foot deterred them so long that the habit of not going is too strong to overcome. And then if they did go, who would tend the ever-present baby in arms, the ever-numerous children; make the garden and weed and hoe the young corn for the absent lord and master. I suppose it was generations of just such lonely women, waiting at their cabins in pioneer days for the men to come home, that gives the mountain-woman the brooding look of pathos that so touches the stranger's heart to-day; and it is the watching to-day that will keep unchanged that look of vacant sadness for generations to come.

"Ease her up now!" called old Ben—we were making our first turn—and big Tom at the bow, and young Ben and the scholar at the stern oar, swept the white saplings through the water with a terrific swish. Footholes had been cut along the logs, and in these the men stuck their toes as they pushed, with both hands on the oar and the oar across their breasts. At the end of the stroke, they threw the oar down and up with rhythm and dash. Then they went back on a run to begin another stroke.

"Ease her up—ease her up," said old Ben, soothingly, and then, suddenly:

"Hit her up—hit her up—hell!"

Solemn Tim began to look ashore for a good place to jump. The bow barely slipped past the bend of the river.

"That won't do," said old Ben again; "Hell!" Big Tom looked as crestfallen as a school-boy, and said nothing—we had just escaped "bowing" on our first turn. Ten minutes later we swept into the Narrows—the "Nahrers" as the mountaineer says; and it was quick and dangerous work keeping the unwieldy craft from striking a bowlder, or the solid wall of a vertical cliff that on either side rose straight upward, for the river was pressed into a narrow channel, and ran with terrific force. It was one long exhilarating thrill going through those Narrows, and everybody looked relieved when we slipped out of them into broad water, which ran straight for half a mile—where the oars were left motionless and the men got back their breath and drew their pipes and bottles. I knew the innocent white liquor that revenue man and mountaineer call "moonshine," and a wary sip or two was enough for me. Along with the bottle came the inevitable first question that,

under any and all circumstances, every mountaineer asks the stranger, no matter if the
stranger has asked him a question first.

"Well, stranger, what mought yo' name
be?"

Answering that, you are expected to tell in
the same breath, as well, what your business is.
I knew it was useless to tell mine—it would
not have been understood, and would have en-
gendered suspicion. I was at Jackson; I had
long wanted to go down the river on a raft, and
I let them think that I was going for curiosity
and fun; but I am quite sure they were not
wholly satisfied until I had given them ground
to believe that I could afford the trip for fun,
by taking them up to the hotel that night for
supper, and giving them some very bad cigars.
For, though the moon was full, the sky was
black with clouds, and old Ben said we must tie
up for the night. That tying up was exciting
work. The raft was worked cautiously toward
the shore, and a man stood at bow and stern
with a rope, waiting his chance to jump ashore
and coil it about a tree. Tom jumped first, and
I never realized what the momentum of the raft
was until I saw him, as he threw the rope about a
tree, jerked like a straw into the bushes, the rope
torn from his hands, and heard the raft crashing
down through the undergrowth. Tom gave

chase along the bank, and everybody yelled and
ran to and fro. It was crash—swish—bump—
grind and crash again; and it was only by the
hardest work at the clumsy oars that we kept
the raft off the shore. From a rock Tom made
a flying leap aboard again, and luckily the river
broadened there, and just past the point of a
thicket we came upon another raft already
anchored. The boy Ben picked up his rope
and prepared to leap aboard the stranger,
from the other end of which a mountaineer ran
toward us.

"Keep off," he shouted, "keep off, I tell ye,"
but the boy paid no attention, and the other
man pulled his pistol. Ben dropped his rope,
then looked around, laughed, picked up his rope
again and jumped aboard. The fellow lowered
his pistol and swore. I looked around, too,
then. Every man on board with us had his pistol in his hand. We tugged the stranger's cable
sorely, but it held him fast and he held us fast,
and the tying up was done.

"He'd 'a' done us the same way," said old
Ben, in palliation.

Next day it was easy sailing most of the time,
and we had long rests from the oars, and we
smoked, and the bottles were slowly emptied, one
by one, while the mountaineers " jollied " each
other and told drawling stories. Once we struck

a long eddy, and were caught by it and swept back up-stream; twice this happened before we could get in the current again. Then they all laughed and " jollied " old Ben.

It seemed that the old fellow had taken too much one dark night and had refused to tie up. There was a house at the head of this eddy, and when he struck it there was a gray horse hitched to the fence outside; and inside was the sound of fiddles and furious dancing. Next morning old Ben told another raftsman that he had seen more gray horses and heard nor iddling that night than he had see and heard since he was born.

" They was a-fiddlin' an' a-dancin' at every house I passed last night," he said, " an I'm damned if I didn't see a gray hoss hitched outside every time I heerd the fiddlin'. I reckon they was ha'nts." The old fellow laughed good-naturedly while the scholar was telling his story. He had been caught in the eddy and had been swung around and around, passing the same house and the same horse each time.

I believe I have remarked that those bottles were emptying fast. By noon they were quite empty, and two hours later, as we rounded a curve, the scholar went to the bow, put his hands to his mouth and shouted:

" Whis-kee! "

And again:

" Whiss-kee-ee! "

A girl sprang from the porch of a cabin far down the stream, and a moment later a canoe was pushed from the bushes, and the girl, standing erect, paddled it up-stream close to the bank and shot it out alongside the raft.

" Howdye, Mandy! "

" Howdye, boys! "

Young Ben took two bottles from her, gave her some pieces of silver, and, as we sped on, she turned shoreward again and stood holding the bushes and looking after us, watching young Ben, as he was watching her; for she was black-eyed and pretty.

The sky was broken with hardly a single cloud that night. The moon was yellow as a flame, and we ran all night long. I lay with my feet to the fire that Ben had built on some stones in the middle of the raft, looking up at the trees that arched over us, and the steep, moonlit cliffs, and the moon itself riding high and full and so brilliant that the stars seemed to have fallen in a shower all around the horizon. The raft ran as noiselessly as a lily-pad, and it was all as still and wild as a dream. Once or twice we heard the yelp of a fox-hound and the yell of a hunter out in the hills, and the mountaineers yelled back in answer and hied the dog on. Sometimes young Ben and the scholar, and even solemn Tim, sang some weird old ballad that one can hear now only in the Southern hills; and twice, to my delight and surprise, the scholar "yodelled." I wondered where he had learned how. He did not know—he had always known how. It was perhaps only another of the curious Old World survivals that are of ceaseless interest to a speculative "furriner," and was no stranger than the songs he sang. I went to sleep by and by, and woke up shivering. It was yet dark, but signs of day were evident; and in the dim light I could see young Ben at the stern-oar on watch, and the huge shape of big Tom standing like a statue at the bow and peering ahead. We had made good time during the night—the mountaineers say a raft makes better time during the night—why, I could not see, nor could they explain, and at daybreak we were sweeping around the hills of the brush country, and the scholar who had pointed out things of interest (he was a school-teacher at home) began to show his parts with some pride. Every rock and cliff and turn and eddy down that long river has some picturesque name that the river-men have given it—names known only to them. Two rocks that shoved their black shoulders up on either side of the stream have been called Buck and Billy, after some old fellow's favorite oxen, for more than half a century. Here was an eagle's nest. A bear had been seen not long ago, looking from a black hole in the face of a cliff. How he got there no one could understand. The scholar told some strong stories—now that we were in a region of historical interest—where Boone planted his first fort and where Boonesborough once stood, but he always prefaced his tale with the overwhelming authority that:

" Hist'ry says! "

He declared that history said that a bull, seeing some cows across the river, had jumped from the point of a high cliff straight down into the river; had swum across and fallen dead as he was climbing the bank.

" He busted his heart," said the scholar.

Oddly enough, solemn Tim, who had never cracked a smile, was the first to rebel.

" You see that cliff yander? " said the scholar. " Well, hist'ry says that Dan'l Boone druv three Injuns once straight over that cliff down into the river."

I could see that Tim was loath to cast discredit on the facts of history. If the scholar had said one or even two Indians, I don't think Tim would have called a halt; but for Daniel, with only one load in his gun—and it not a Winchester—to drive *three*—it was too much.

And yet Tim never smiled, and it was the first time I heard him voluntarily open his lips.

"Well, hist'ry mought 'a' said that," he said, "but I reckon *Dan'l was in the lead!*" The yell that went up routed the scholar and stilled him. History said no farther down that stream, even when we were passing between the majestic cliffs that in one place are spanned by the third highest bridge in the world. There a ferry was crossing the river, and old Ben grew reminiscential. He had been a ferryman back in the mountains.

"Thar was a slosh of ice runnin' in the river," he said, " an' a feller come a-lopin' down the road one day, an' hollered an' axed me to take him across. I knowed from his voice that he was a-drinkin', and I hollered back an' axed him if he was drunk.

"'Yes, I'm drunk!'

"'How drunk?' I says.

"'Drunk as hell!' he says, 'but I can ride that boat.'

"Well, there was a awful slosh o' ice a-runnin', but I let him on, an' we hadn't got more'n ten feet from the bank when that feller fell off in that slosh o' ice. Well, I ketched him by one foot, an' I drug him an' I drug him an' I drug his face about twenty feet in the mud, an' do you know that damn fool come might' nigh a-drownin' before I could *change eends!* "

Thence on, the trip was monotonous except for the Kentuckian who loves every blade of grass in his land—for we struck locks and dams and smooth and slower water, and the hills were low but high enough to shut off the blue-grass fields. But we knew they were there—slope and woodland, bursting into green—and the trip from highland to lowland, barren hillside to rich pasture-land—from rhododendron to blue-grass—was done.

At dusk that day we ran slowly into the little Kentucky capital, past distilleries and brick factories with tall smoking stacks and under the big bridge and, wonder of wonders to Ben, past a little stern-wheel steamboat wheezing up-stream. We climbed the bank into the town, where the boy Ben and solemn Tim were for walking single file in the middle of the streets until called by the scholar to the sidewalk. The boy's eyes grew big with wonder when he saw streets and houses of stone, and heard the whistles of factories and saw what was to him a crush of people in the sleepy little town. I parted from them that night, but next morning I saw big Tom passing the station on foot. He said his companions had taken his things and gone on by train, and that he was going to walk back. I wondered, and while I asked no questions, I should like to wager that I guessed the truth. Tom had spent every cent of his money for the girl in crimson homespun who was waiting for him away back in the hills, and if I read her face aright I could have told him that she would have given every trinket he had sent her rather than wait a day longer for the sight of his face. We shook hands, and I watched him pass out of sight with his face set homeward across and beyond the blue-grass, through the brush country and the Indian Old Fields, back to his hills of laurel and rhododendron.

THROUGH THE BAD BEND

THROUGH THE BAD BEND

A WILDLY beautiful cleft through the Cumberland Range opens into the head of Powell's Valley, in Virginia, and forms the Gap. From this point a party of us were going bass-fishing on a fork of the Cumberland River over in the Kentucky mountains. It was Sunday, and several Kentucky mountaineers had crossed over that day to take their first ride on the cars, and to see " the city "—as the Gap has been prophetically called ever since it had a cross-roads store, one little hotel, two farm-houses, and a blacksmith's shop. From them we learned that we could ride down Powell's Valley and get to the fork of the Cumberland by simply climbing over the mountain. As the mountaineers were going back home the same day, Breck and I boarded the train with them, intending to fish down the fork of the river to the point where the rest of the party would strike the same stream, two days later.

At the second station down the road a crowd of Virginia mountaineers got on board. Most of them had been drinking, and the festivities soon began. One drunken young giant pulled his revolver, swung it back over his shoulder— the muzzle almost grazing a woman's face behind him—and swung it up again to send a bullet crashing through the top of the car. The hammer was at the turning-point when a companion caught his wrist. At the same time, the fellow's sister sprang across the aisle, and, wrenching the weapon from his grasp, hid it in her dress. Simultaneously his partner at the other end of the car was drawing a .45 Colt's half as long as his arm. A quick panic ran through the car, and in a moment there was no one in it with us but the mountaineers, the conductor, one brakeman, and one other man, who sat still in his seat, with one hand under his coat. The prospect was neither pleasant nor peaceful, and we rose to our feet and waited. The disarmed giant was raging through the aisle searching and calling, with mighty oaths, for his pistol. The other had backed into a corner of the car, waving his revolver, turning his head from side to side to avoid a surprise in the rear, white with rage, and just drunk enough to shoot. The little conductor was unmoved and smiling, and, by some quiet mesmerism, he kept the two in subjection until the station was reached.

The train moved out and left us among the

drunken maniacs, no house in sight, the darkness settling on us, and the unclimbed mountain looming up into it. The belligerents paid no attention to us, however, but disappeared quickly, with an occasional pistol-shot and a yell from the bushes, each time sounding farther away. The Kentucky mountaineers were going to climb the mountain. A storm was coming, but there was nothing else to do. So we shouldered our traps and followed them.

There were eight of us—an old man and his two daughters, the husband of one of these, the sweetheart of the other, and a third man, who showed suspicion of us from the beginning. This man with a flaring torch led the way; the old man followed him, and there were two mountaineers deep between the girls and us, who went last.

It was not long before a ragged line of fire cut through the blackness overhead, and the thunder began to crash and the rain to fall. The torch was beaten out, and for a moment there was a halt. Breck and I could hear a muffled argument going on in the air above us, and, climbing toward the voices, we felt the lintel of a mountain-cabin and heard a long drawl of welcome.

The cabin was one dark room without even a loft, the home of a newly married pair. They themselves had evidently just gotten home, for the hostess was on her knees at the big fireplace, blowing a few coals into a blaze. The rest of us sat on the two beds in the room waiting for the fire-light, and somebody began talking about the trouble on the train.

" Did you see that feller settin' thar with his hand under his coat while Jim was tryin' to shoot the brakeman? " said one. " Well, Jim killed his brother a year ago, an' the feller was jus' waitin' fer a chance to git Jim right then. I knowed that."

"Who was the big fellow who started the row, by flourishing his pistol around? " I asked.

A man on the next bed leaned forward and laughed slightly. " Well, stranger, I reckon that was me."

This sounds like the opening chapter of a piece of fiction, but we had really stumbled upon this man's cabin in the dark, and he was our host. A little spinal chill made me shiver. He had not seen us yet, and I began to wonder whether he would recognize us when the light blazed up, and whether he would know that we were ready to take part against him in the car, and what would happen, if he did. When the blaze did kindle, he was reaching for his hip, but he drew out a bottle of apple-jack and handed it over the foot of the bed.

"Somebody ought to 'a' knocked my head off," he said.

"That's so," said the younger girl, with sharp boldness. "I never seed sech doin's."

The old mountaineer, her father, gave her a quick rebuke, but the man laughed. He was sobering up, and, apparently, he had never seen us before. The young wife prepared supper, and we ate and went to bed—the ten of us in that one room. The two girls took off their shoes and stockings with frank innocence, and warmed their bare feet at the fire. The host and hostess gave up their bed to the old mountaineer and his son-in-law, and slept, like the rest of us, on the floor.

We were wakened long before day. Indeed it was pitch dark when, after a mountain custom, we stumbled to a little brook close to the cabin and washed our faces. A wood-thrush was singing somewhere in the darkness, and its cool notes had the liquid freshness of the morning. We did not wait for breakfast, so anxious were the Kentuckians to get home, or so fearful were they of abusing their host's hospitality, though the latter urged us strenuously to stay. Not a cent would he take from anybody, and I know now that he was a moonshiner, a feudsman, an outlaw, and that he was running from the sheriff at that very time.

With a parting pull at the apple-jack, we began, on an empty stomach, that weary climb. Not far up the mountain Breck stopped, panting, while the mountaineers were swinging on up the path without an effort, even the girls; but Breck swore that he had heart disease, and must rest. When I took part of his pack, the pretty one looked back over her shoulder and smiled at him without scorn. Both were shy, and had not spoken a dozen words with either of us. Half-way up we overtook a man and a boy, one carrying a tremendous demijohn and the other a small hand-barrel. They had been over on the Virginia side selling moonshine, and I saw the light of gladness in Breck's eye, for his own flask was wellnigh empty from returning our late host's courtesy. But both man and boy disappeared with a magical suddenness that became significant later. Already we were suspected as being revenue spies, though neither of us dreamed what the matter was.

We reached the top after daybreak, and the beauty of the sunrise over still seas of white mist and wave after wave of blue Virginia hills was unspeakable, as was the beauty of the descent on the Kentucky side, down through primeval woods of majestic oak and poplar, under a trembling world of dew-drenched leaves, and along a tumbling series of waterfalls that flashed through tall ferns, blossoming laurel, and shining leaves of rhododendron.

The sun was an hour high when we reached the foot of the mountain. There the old man and the young girl stopped at a little cabin where lived the son-in-law. We, too, were pressed to stop, but we went on with the suspicious one to his house, where we got breakfast. There the people took pay, for their house was weather-boarded, and they were more civilized; or perhaps for the reason that the man thought us spies. I did not like his manner, and I got the first unmistakable hint of his suspicions after breakfast. I was down behind the barn, and he and another mountaineer came down on the other side.

" Didn't one o' them fellers come down this way? " I heard him ask.

I started to make my presence known, but he spoke too quickly, and I concluded it was best to keep still.

" No tellin' whut them damn fellers is up to. I don't like their occupation."

That is, we were the first fishermen to cast a minnow with a reel into those waters, and it was beyond the mountaineer's comprehension to understand how two men could afford to come so far and spend time and a little money just for the fun of fishing. They supposed we were

203

fishing for profit, and later they asked us how we kept our fish fresh, and how we got them over the mountain, and where we sold them. With this idea, naturally it was a puzzle to them how we could afford to give a boy a quarter for a dozen minnows, and then, perhaps, catch not a single fish with them.

When I got back to the house, Breck was rigging his rod, with a crowd of spectators around him. Such a rod and such a fisherman had never been seen in that country before. Breck was dressed in a white tennis-shirt, blue gymnasium breeches, blue stockings, and white tennis-shoes. With a cap on his shock of black hair and a .38 revolver in his belt, he was a thing for those women to look at and to admire, and for the men to scorn—secretly, of course, for there was a look in his black eyes that forced guarded respect in any crowd. The wonder of those mountaineers when he put his rod together, fastened the reel, and tossed his hook fifty feet in the air was worth the morning's climb to see. At the same time they made fun of our rods, and laughed at the idea of getting out a big " green pyerch "—as the mountaineers call bass — with " them switches." Their method is to tie a strong line to a long hickory sapling, and, when they strike a bass, to put the stout pole over one shoulder and walk ashore with it. Before the sun was over the mountain, we were wading down the stream, while two boys carried our minnows and clothes along the bank. The news of our coming went before us, and every now and then a man would roll out of the bushes with a gun and look at us with much suspicion and some wonder. For two luckless hours we cast down that too narrow and too shallow stream before we learned that there was a dam two miles farther down, and at once we took the land for it. It was after dinner when we reached it, and there the boys left us. We could not induce them to go farther. An old miller sat outside his mill across the river, looking at us with some curiosity, but no surprise, for the coming of a stranger in those mountains is always known miles ahead of him.

We told him our names and that we were from Virginia, but were natives of the Bluegrass, and we asked if he could give us dinner. His house was half a mile farther down the river, he said, but the women folks were at home, and he reckoned they would give us something to eat. When we started, I shifted my revolver from my pocket to a kodak-camera case that I had brought along to hold fishing-tackle.

"I suppose I can put this thing in here?" I

said to Breck, not wanting to risk arrest for carrying concealed weapons and the confiscation of the pistol, which was valuable. Breck hesitated, and the old miller studied us keenly.

" Well," he said, " if you two air from Kanetucky, hit strikes me you ought to know the laws of yo' own State. You can carry it in thar as baggage," he added, quietly, and I knew that my question had added another fagot to the flame of suspicion kindling against us.

In half an hour we were in the cool shade of a spreading apple-tree in the miller's yard, with our bare feet in thick, cool grass, while the miller's wife and his buxom, red-cheeked daughter got us dinner. And a good dinner it was; and we laughed and cracked jokes at each other till the sombre, suspicious old lady relaxed and laughed, too, and the girl lost some of her timidity and looked upon Breck with wide-eyed admiration, while Breck ogled back outrageously.

After dinner a scowling mountaineer led a mule through the yard and gave us a surly nod. Two horsemen rode up to the gate and waited to escort us down the river. One of them carried our baggage, for no matter what he suspects, the mountaineer will do anything in the world for a stranger until the moment of actual conflict comes. In our green innocence, we thought it rather a good joke that we should be

taken for revenue men, so that, Breck's flask
being empty, he began by telling one of the men
that we had been wading the river all the morning, that the water was cold, and that, anyway,
a little swallow now and then often saved a fellow from a cold and fever. He had not been
able to get any from anybody—and couldn't
the man *do* something? The mountaineer was
touched, and he took the half-dollar that Breck
gave him, and turned it over, with a whispered
consultation, to one of two more horsemen that
we met later on the road. Still farther on we
found a beautiful hole of water, edged with a
smooth bank of sand—a famous place, the men
told us, for green "pyerch." Mountaineers
rolled out of the bushes to watch us while we
were rigging up, some with guns and some without. We left our pistols on the shore, and several examined them curiously, especially mine,
which was hammerless. Later, I showed them
how it worked, and explained that one advantage of it was that, in close quarters, the other
man could not seize your pistol, get his finger or
thumb under your hammer, and prevent you
from shooting at all. This often happens in a
fight, of course, and the point appealed to them
strongly, but I could see that they were wondering why I should be carrying a gun that was
good for close quarters, since close quarters are

rarely necessary except in case of making arrests. Pretty soon the two men who had gone for Breck's " moonshine " returned, and a gleam rose in Breck's eye and went quickly down. Instead of a bottle, the boy handed back the half-dollar.

" I couldn't git any," he said. He lied, of course, as we both knew, and the disappointment in Breck's face was so sincere that his companion, with a gesture that was half sympathy, half defiance, whisked a bottle from his hip.

" Well, by —— I'll give him a drink! "

It was fiery, white as water, and so fresh that we could taste the smoke in it, but it was good, and we were grateful. All the afternoon, from two to a dozen people watched us fish, but we had poor luck, which is never a surprise, fishing for bass. Perhaps the fish had gone to nesting, or the trouble may have been the light of the moon, during which they feed all night, and are not so hungry through the day; or it may have been any of the myriad reasons that make the mystery and fascination of catching bass. At another time, and from the same stream, I have seen two rods take out one hundred bass, ranging from one to five pounds in weight, in a single day. An hour by sun, we struck for the house of the old man with whom we had crossed the mountain, and, that night, we learned that we had passed through a locality alive with moonshiners, and banded together with such system and determination that the revenue agents rarely dared to make a raid on them. We were supposed to be two spies who were expected to come in there that spring. We had passed within thirty yards of a dozen stills, and our host hinted where we might find them. We thanked him, and told him we preferred to keep as far away from them as possible. He was much puzzled. He also said that we had been in the head-quarters of a famous desperado, who was the leader of the Howard faction in the famous Howard-Turner feud. He was a non-combatant himself, but he had " feelin's," as he phrased it, for the other side. He was much surprised when we told him we were going back there next day. We had told the people we were coming back, and next morning we were foolish enough to go.

As soon as we struck the river, we saw a man with a Winchester sitting on a log across the stream, as though his sole business in life was to keep an eye on us. All that day we were never out of sight of a mountaineer and a gun; we never had been, I presume, since our first breakfast on that stream. Still, everybody was kind and hospitable and honest—how honest this incident will show. An old woman cooked dinner especially for us, and I gave her two quarters. She took them, put them away, and while she sat smoking her pipe, I saw something was troubling her. She got up presently, went into a room, came back, and without a word dropped one of the quarters into my hand. Half a dollar was too much. They gave us moonshine, too, and Breck remarked casually that we were expecting to meet our friends at Uncle Job Turner's, somewhere down the river. They would have red whiskey from the Blue-grass and we would be all right. Then he asked how far down Uncle Job lived. The remark and the question occasioned very badly con-cealed excitement, and I wondered what had happened, but I did not ask. I was getting wary, and I had become quite sure that the fish-ing must be better down, very far down, that stream. When we started again, the moun-taineers evidently held a quick council of war. One can hear a long distance over water at the quiet of dusk, and they were having a lively dis-cussion about us and our business over there. Somebody was defending us, and I recognized the voice as belonging to a red-whiskered fel-low, who said he had lived awhile in the Blue-grass, and had seen young fellows starting to the Kentucky River to fish for fun. " Oh, them damn fellers ain't up to nothin'," we could hear him say, with the disgust of the cosmopolitan. " I tell ye, they lives in town an' they likes to git out this way! "

I have always believed that this man saved us trouble right then, for next night the mountaineers came down in a body to the house where we had last stopped. But we had gone on rather hastily, and when we reached Uncle Job Turner's, the trip behind us became more interesting than ever in retrospect. All along we asked where Uncle Job lived, and once we shouted the question across the river, where some women and boys were at work, weeding corn. As usual, the answer was another question, and always the same—what were our names? Breck yelled, in answer, that we were from Virginia, and that they would be no wiser if we should tell—an answer that will always be unwise in the mountains of Kentucky as long as moonshine is made and feuds survive. We asked again, and another yell told us that the next house was Uncle Job's. The next house was rather pretentious. It had two or three rooms, apparently, and a loft, and was weather-boarded; but it was as silent as a tomb. We shouted " Hello! " from outside the fence, which is etiquette in the mountains. Not a sound. We shouted again—once, twice, many times. It was most strange. Then

we waited, and shouted again, and at last a big
gray-haired old fellow slouched out and asked
rather surlily what we wanted.

" Dinner."

He seemed pleased that that was all, and his
manner changed immediately. His wife appeared; then, as if by magic, two or three children, one a slim, wild, dark-eyed girl of fifteen,
dressed in crimson homespun. As we sat on the
porch I saw her passing through the dark rooms,
but always, while we were there, if I entered one
door she slipped out of the other. Breck was
more fortunate. He came up behind her the
next day at sundown while she was dancing bare-
footed in the dust of the road, driving her cows
home. Later I saw him in the cow-pen, helping
her milk. He said she was very nice, but very
shy.

We got dinner, and the old man sent after a
bottle of moonshine, and in an hour he was
thawed out wonderfully.

We told him where we had been, and as he
slowly began to believe us, he alternately grew
sobered and laughed aloud.

" Went through thar fishin', did ye? Wore
yo' pistols? Axed whar thar was branches whar
you could ketch minners? Oh, Lawd! Didn't
ye know that the stills air al'ays up the branches?
Tol' 'em you was goin' to *meet a party at my*

house, and stay here awhile fishin'? Oh, Lawdy! Ef that ain't a good un!"

We didn't see it, but we did later, when we knew that we had come through the "Bad Bend," which was the head-quarters of the Howard leader and his chief men; that Uncle Job was the most prominent man of the other faction, and lived farthest up the river of all the Turners; that he hadn't been up in the Bend for ten years, and that we had given his deadly enemies the impression that we were friends of his. As Uncle Job grew mellow, and warmed up in his confidences, something else curious came out. Every now and then he would look at me and say:

"I seed you lookin' at my pants." And then he would throw back his head and laugh. After he had said this for the third time, I did look at his "pants," and I saw that he was soaking wet to the thighs—why, I soon learned. A nephew of his had killed a man at the county-seat only a week before. Uncle Job had gone on his bond. When we shouted across the river, he was in the cornfield, and when we did not tell our names, he got suspicious, and, mistaking our rod-holders for guns, had supposed that his nephew had run away, and that we were officers come to arrest him. He had run down the river on the other side, had waded the stream, and was up in the loft with his Winchester on us while we were shouting at his gate. He told us this very frankly. Nor would even he believe that we were fishing. He, too, thought that we were officers looking through the Bad Bend for some criminal, and the least innocent mission that struck him as plausible was that, perhaps, we might be looking over the ground to locate a railroad, or prospecting for coal veins. When Uncle Job went down the road with us the next morning, he took his wife along, so that no Howard would try to ambush him through fear of hitting a woman. And late that afternoon, when we were fishing with Uncle Job's son in some thick bushes behind the house, some women passed along in the path above us, and, seeing us, but not seeing him, scurried out of sight as though frightened. Little Job grinned.

"Them women thinks the Howards have hired you fellers to layway dad."

The next morning I lost Breck, and about noon I got a note from him, written with a trembling lead-pencil, to the effect that he believed he would fish up a certain creek that afternoon. As the creek was not more than three feet wide and a few inches deep, I knew what had happened, and I climbed one of Job's mules and went to search for him. Breck had stumbled upon a moonshine still, and, getting hilarious, had climbed a barrel and was making to a crowd of mountaineers a fiery political speech. Breck had captured that creek, "wild-cat" still and all, and to this day I never meet a mountaineer from that region who does not ask, with a wide grin, about Breck.

When we reached the county-seat, the next day, we met the revenue deputy. He said the town was talking about two spies who were up the Fork. We told him that we must be the spies. The old miller was the brains of the Bend, he said, both in outwitting the revenue men and in planning the campaign of the Howard leader against the Turners, and he told us of several fights he had had in the Bad Bend. He said that we were lucky to come through alive; that what saved us was sticking to the river, hiring our minnows caught, leaving our pistols on the bank to be picked up by anybody, the defence of the red-whiskered man from the Blue-grass, and Breck's popularity at the still. I thought he was exaggerating—that the mountaineers, even if convinced that we were spies, would have given us a chance to get out of the country—but when he took me over to a room across the street and showed me where his predecessor, a man whom I had known quite well, was shot through a window at night and killed, I was not quite so sure.

But still another straw of suspicion was awaiting us. When we reached the railroad again—by another route, you may be sure—Breck, being a lawyer, got permission for us to ride on a freight-train, and thus save a night and a day. The pass for us was technically charged to the mail service. The captain and crew of the train were overwhelmingly and mysteriously polite to us—an inexplicable contrast to the surliness with which passengers are usually treated on a freight-train. When we got off at the Gap, and several people greeted us by name, the captain laughed.

"Do you know what these boys thought you two were?" he asked, referring to his crew. "They thought you were freight 'spotters.'"

The crew laughed. I looked at Breck, and I didn't wonder. He was a ragged, unshaven tramp, and I was another.

Months later, I got a message from the Bad Bend. Breck and I mustn't come through there any more. We have never gone through there any more, though anybody on business that the mountaineers understand, *can* go more safely than he can cross Broadway at Twenty-third Street, at noon. As a matter of fact, however, there are two other forks to the Cumberland in which the fishing is very good indeed, and just now I would rather risk Broadway.

TO THE BREAKS OF SANDY

TO THE BREAKS OF SANDY

DOWN in the southwestern corner of Virginia, and just over the Kentucky line, are the Gap and " The Gap "—the one made by nature and the other by man. One is a ragged gash down through the Cumberland Mountains, from peak to water level; and the other is a new little, queer little town, on a pretty plateau which is girdled by two running streams that loop and come together like the framework of an ancient lute. Northeast the range runs, unbroken by nature and undisturbed by man, until it crumbles at the Breaks of Sandy, seventy miles away. There the bass leaps from rushing waters, and there, as nowhere else this side of the Rockies, is the face of nature wild and shy.

It was midsummer, the hour was noon, and we were bound for the Breaks of Sandy, seventy miles away.

No similar aggregate of man, trap, and beast had ever before penetrated those mountain wilds. The wagon was high-seated and the team was spiked, with Rock and Ridgling as wheel horses, Diavolo as leader, and Dolly, a half thorough-

bred, galloping behind under Sam, the black
cook, and a wild Western saddle, with high
pommels, heavily hooded stirrups, hand-worked
leather, and multitudinous straps and shaking
rawhide strings; and running alongside, Tiger,
bull-terrier. Any man who was at Andover,
Cornell, or Harvard during certain years will, if
he sees these lines, remember Tiger.

As for the men—there was Josh, ex-captain
of a Kentucky Horse Guard, ex-captain of the
volunteer police force back at " The Gap," and,
like Henry Clay, always captain whenever and
wherever there was anything to be done and
more than one man was needed to do it; now,
one of the later-day pioneers who went back over
the Cumberland, not many years ago, to reclaim
a certain wild little corner of old Virginia, and
then, as now, the first man and the leading lawyer of the same. There was another Kentuckian, fresh from the Blue-grass—Little Willie, as
he was styled on this trip—being six feet three
in his bare feet, carrying 190 pounds of bone
and muscle; champion heavy-weight with his
fists in college (he could never get anybody to
fight with him), centre-rush in foot-ball, with
this grewsome record of broken bones: collar-
bone, one leg, one knee three times, and three
teeth smashed—smashed by biting through his
nose guard against each other when he set his

jaws to break through a hostile line. Also, Willie was ex-bugler of a military school, singer of coon songs unrivalled, and with other accomplishments for which there is no space here to record. There was Dan, boy-manager of a mighty coal company, good fellow, and of importance to the dog-lover as the master of Tiger. I include Tiger here, because he was so little less than human. There are no words to describe Tiger. He was prepared for Yale at Andover, went to Cornell in a pet, took a postgraduate course at Harvard, and, getting indifference and world-weariness there, followed his master to pioneer in the Cumberland. Tiger has a white collar, white-tipped tail, white feet; his body is short, strong, close-knit, tawny, ringed; and his peculiar distinctions are intelligence, character, magnetism. All through the mountains Tiger has run his fifty miles a day behind Dolly, the thorough-bred; so that, in a radius of a hundred miles, there is nobody who does not know that dog. Still, he never walks unless it is necessary, and his particular oscillation is between the mines and " The Gap," ten miles apart. Being a coal magnate, he has an annual pass and he always takes the train— alone, if he pleases—changing cars three times and paying no attention, until his stations are called. Sometimes he is too weary to go to a station, so he sits down on the track and waits for the train. I have known the engineer of a heavily laden freight train to slacken up when he saw Tiger trotting ahead between the rails, and stop to take him aboard, did Tiger but nod at him. I have never seen man, woman, or child, of respectable antecedents, whom that dog didn't love, and nobody, regardless of antecedents, who didn't love that dog.

Such, we rattled out of " The Gap " that midsummer noon. Northward, through the Gap, a cloud of dun smoke hung over the Hades of coke ovens that Dan had planted in the hills. On the right was the Ridge, heavy with beds of ore. Straight ahead was a furnace, from which the coke rose as pale-blue smoke and the ore gave out a stream of molten iron. Farther on, mountains to the right and mountains to the left came together at a little gap, and toward that point we rattled up Powell's Valley—smiling back at the sun; furnace, ore-mine, coke-cloud, and other ugly signs of civilization dropping behind us fast, and our eyes set toward one green, lovely spot that was a shrine of things primeval.

In the wagon we had a tent, and things to eat, and a wooden box that looked like a typewriter case, under lock and key, and eloquently inscribed:

" Glass, 2 gal." It is a great way to carry the

indispensable—in a wagon—and I recommend it to fishermen.

At the foot of the first mountain was a spring and we stopped to water the horses and unlock that case. Twenty yards above, and to one side of the road, a mountaineer was hanging over the fence, looking down at us.

" Have a drink? " said Josh.

" Yes," he drawled, " if ye'll fetch it up."

" Come an' get it," said Josh, shortly.

" Are you sick? " I asked.

" Sort o' puny."

We drank.

" Have a drink? " said Josh once more.

" If ye'll fetch it up."

Josh drove the cork home with the muscular base of his thumb.

" I'm damned if I do."

Dan whistled to Diavolo, and we speculated. It was queer conduct in the mountaineer—why didn't he come down?

" I don't know," said Dan.

" He really came down for a drink," I said, knowing the mountaineer's independence, " and he wanted to prove to himself and to us that he didn't."

" A smart Alec," said Little Willie.

" A plain damn fool," said Josh.

Half an hour later we were on top of the

mountain, in the little gap where the mountains came together. Below us the valley started on its long, rich sweep southward, and beyond were the grim shoulders of Black Mountains, which we were to brush now and then on our way to the " Breaks."

There Dan put Tiger out of the wagon and made him walk. After three plaintive whines to his master to show cause for such an outrage, Tiger dropped nose and eyes to the ground and jogged along with such human sullenness that Willie was led to speak to him. Tiger paid no attention. I called him and Dan called him. Tiger never so much as lifted eye or ear, and Willie watched him, wondering.

" Why, that dog's got a grouch," he said at last, delightedly. " I tell you he's got a grouch." It was Willie's first observation of Tiger. Of course he had a " grouch " as distinctly as a child who is old enough to show petulance with dignity. And having made us feel sufficiently mean, Tiger dropped quite behind, as though to say: " I'm gettin' kind o' tired o' this. Now 'It's come here, Tiger,' and 'Stick in the mud, Tiger,' and straightway again, 'Tiger, come here.' I don't like it. I'd go home if it weren't for Dolly and this nigger here, whom I reckon I've got to watch. But I'll stick in the mud." And he did.

At dusk we passed through Norton, where Talt Hall, desperado, killed his thirteenth and last man, and on along a rocky, muddy, Stygian-black road to Wise Court-house, where our police guard from " The Gap," with Josh as captain, guarded Talt for one month to keep his Kentucky clan from rescuing him. And there we told Dan and the big Kentuckian how banker, broker, lawyer, and doctor left his business and his home, cut port-holes in the court-house, put the town under martial law, and, with twenty men with Winchesters in the rude box that enclosed the scaffold, and a cordon of a hundred more in a circle outside, to keep back a thousand mountaineers, thus made possible the first hanging that the county had ever known. And how, later, in the same way we hung old Doc Taylor, Hall's enemy— Swedenborgian preacher, herb doctor, revenue officer, and desperado—the " Red Fox of the Mountains."

The two listeners were much interested, for, in truth, that police guard of gentlemen who hewed strictly to the line of the law, who patrolled the streets of " The Gap " with billy, whistle, and pistol, knocking down toughs, lugging them to the calaboose, appearing in court against them next morning, and maintaining a fund for the prosecution of them in the higher courts, was as unique and successful an experiment in civilization as any borderland has ever known.

Next day we ran the crests of long ridges and struck good roads, and it was then that we spiked Rock and Ridgling, with Diavolo as leader.

"Tool 'em!" shouted Willie, and we "tooled" joyously. A coach-horn was all that we lacked, and we did not lack that long. Willie evolved one from his unaided throat, in some mysterious way that he could not explain, but he did the tooting about as well as it is ever done with a horn. It was hot, and the natives stared. They took us for the advance-guard of a circus.

"Where are you goin' to show?" they shouted. We crossed ridges, too, tooling recklessly about the edges of precipices and along roads scarcely wide enough for one wagon — Dan swinging to the brake with one hand and holding Josh in the driver's seat with the other—Willie and I speculating, meanwhile, how much higher the hind wheel could go from the ground before the wagon would overturn. It was great fun, and dangerous.

"Hank Monks is not in it," said Willie.

The brake required both of Dan's hands just then and Josh flew out into space and landed on

They took us for the advance-guard of a circus.

his shoulder, some ten feet down the mountain, unhurt.

Rock, though it was his first work under harness, was steady as a plough-horse. Ridgling now and then would snort and plunge and paw, getting one foot over the wagon tongue. Diavolo, like his master, was a born leader, or we should have had trouble indeed.

That night we struck another county-seat, where the court-house had been a brick bone of contention for many, many years—two localities claiming the elsewhere undisputed honor, for the reason that they alone had the only two level acres in the county on which a court-house could stand. A bitter fight it was, and they do say that not many years ago, in a similar conflict, the opposing factions met to decide the question with fist and skull—150 picked men on each side —a direct and curious survival of the ancient wager of battle. The women prevented the fight. Over in Kentucky there would have been a bloody feud. At that town we had but fitful sleep. Certain little demons of the dark, which shall be nameless, marked us, as they always mark fresh victims, for their own.

" I'll bet they look over the register every-night," said Willie — baring a red-splotched brawny arm next morning.

" Wingless victory! " he said, further.

And then on. Wilder and ever wilder, next day, grew the hills and woods and the slitting chasms between them. First one hind wheel dished—we braced it with hickory saplings. Then the other—we braced that. The harness broke—Dan mended that. A horse cast a shoe —Josh shod him then and there. These two were always tinkering, and were happy. Inefficiency made Willie and me miserable — it was plain that we were to be hewers of wood and drawers of water on that trip, and we were.

And still wilder and ever wilder was the face of Nature, which turned primeval—turned Greek. Willie swore he could see the fleeting shapes of nymphs in the dancing sunlight and shadows under the beeches. Where the cane-rushes shivered and shook along the bank of a creek, it was a satyr chasing a dryad through them; and once—it may have been the tinkle of water—but I was sure I heard her laugh float from a dark little ravine high above, where she had fled to hide. No wonder! We were approaching the most isolated spot, perhaps, this side of the Rockies. If this be hard to believe, listen. Once we stopped at a cabin, and Sam, the black cook, went in for a drink of water. A little girl saw him and was thrown almost into convulsions of terror. She had never seen a negro before. Her mother had told her, doubtless, that the bad man would get her some day and she thought Sam was the devil and that he had come for her. And this in Virginia. I knew there were many white people in Virginia, and all throughout the Cumberland, who had never seen a black man, and why they hate him as they do has always been a mystery, especially as they often grant him social equality, even to the point of eating at the same table with him, though the mountaineer who establishes certain relations with the race that is still tolerated in the South, brings himself into lasting disgrace. Perhaps the hostility reaches back to the time when the poor white saw him a fatal enemy, as a slave, to the white man who must work with his hands. And yet, to say that this competition with the black man, along with a hatred of his aristocratic master, was the reason for the universal Union sentiment of the Southern mountaineer during the war is absurd. Competition ceased nearly a century ago. Negro and aristocrat were forgotten—were long unknown. No historian seems to have guessed that the mountaineer was loyal because of 1776. The fight for the old flag in 1812 and the Mexican War helped, but 1776 was enough to keep him loyal to this day; for to-day, in life, character, customs, speech, and conviction, he is practically what he was then. But a change is coming now, and down in a little hollow we saw, suddenly, a startling sign—a frame house with an upper balcony, and, moving along that balcony, a tall figure in a pink ungirded Mother Hubbard. And, mother of all that is modern, we saw against the doorway below her—a bicycle. We took dinner there and the girl gave me her card. It read:

AMANDA TOLLIVER,

EXECUTRIX TO JOSIAH TOLLIVER.

Only that was not her name. She owned coal lands, was a woman of judgment and business, and realizing that she could not develop them alone, had advertised for a partner in coal, and, I was told, in love as well. Anyhow there were numerous pictures of young men around, and I have a faint suspicion that as we swung over the brow of the hill, we might have been taken for suitors four. She had been to school at the county-seat where we spent the first night, and had thus swung into the stream of Progress. She had live gold fish in a glass tank and jugs with plants growing out of the mouth and out of holes in the sides. And she had a carpet in the parlor and fire-screens of red calico and red plush albums, a birthday book, and, of course, a cottage organ. It was all prophetic, I suppose, and the inevitable American way toward higher things; and it was at once sad and hopeful.

Just over the hill, humanity disappeared again and Nature turned primeval — turned Greek again. And again nymphs and river gods began their play. Pretty soon a dryad took human shape in some blackberry bushes, and Little Willie proceeded to take mythological shape as a faun. We moderns jollied him on the metamorphosis.

The Breaks were just ahead. Somewhere through the green thickness of poplar, oak, and maple, the river lashed and boiled between gray bowlders, eddied and danced and laughed through deep pools, or leaped in waves over long riffles, and we turned toward the low, far sound of its waters. A slip of a bare-footed girl stepped from the bushes and ran down the wood-path, and Willie checked her to engage in unnecessary small talk and to ask questions whereof he knew the answers as well as she— all leading to the final one.

"What's your name?" Unlike her hill-sisters, the girl was not shy.

"Melissa."

Shades of Hymettus, but it was fitting. There were blackberry stains about her red lips. Her eyes had the gloom of deep woods and shone from the darkness of her tumbled hair—tumbled it was, like an oatfield I had seen that morning after a wind and rain storm that swept it all night long.

"Melissa!" Willie said softly, once, twice, three times; and his throat gurgled with poetic delight in the maid and the name. I think he would have said "Prithee" and addressed her some more, but just then a homespun mother veered about the corner of a log cabin, and Melissa fled. Willie thought he had scared her.

"On the way to the Breaks," he said—"my first." We hurried the stricken youth on and pitched camp below the cabin, and on a minnow branch that slipped past low willows and under rhododendrons and dropped in happy waterfalls into the Breaks, where began a vertical turreted ledge, hundreds of feet high, that ran majestically on—miles on.

There Willie at once developed unwonted vim. We needed milk and butter and eggs, so he left me to hew wood and draw water while he strode back to the cabin, and Melissa after them; and he made contracts for the same daily —he would go for them himself—and hired all Melissa's little brothers and sisters to pick blackberries for us.

Then came the first supper in the woods and draughts from the typewriter case, the label of which Willie proceeded to alter, because the level of the fluid was sinking, and as a tribute to Melissa.

"Glass—1 gal."

It takes little to make humor in the woods. Followed sweet pipes under the stars, thickening multitudinously straight overhead, where alone we could see them.

Something was troubling Josh that night and I could see that he hesitated about delivering himself—but he did.

"Have you fellows—er—ever noticed—er —that when men get out in the woods they—er —at once begin to swear?" Each one of us had noticed that fact. Josh looked severely at me and severely at Dan and at Willie—not observing that we were looking severely at him.

"Well," he said, with characteristic decision, "I think you ought to stop it."

There was a triangular howl of derision.

"We?" I said.

"We!" said Dan.

"*We*!" yelled Willie.

Josh laughed—he had not heard the rattling fire of picturesque expletives that he had been turning loose on Rock and Ridgling since we left the Gap.

However, we each agreed to be watchful— of the others.

By the by, Willie knocked the ashes from his pipe and picked up a pail—the mother's pail in which he had brought the milk down to camp.

" I reckon they'll need this," he said, thoughtfully. " Don't you think they'll need this? " I was sure they would, and as Willie's colossal shoulders disappeared through the bushes we chuckled, and at the fire Sam, the black cook, snickered respectfully. Willie did not know the lark habits of the mountaineer. We could have told him that Melissa was in bed, but we wickedly didn't. He was soon back, and looking glum. We chuckled some more.

That night a snake ran across my breast—I suppose it was a snake—a toad beat a tattoo on Willie's broad chest, a horse got tangled in the guy-ropes, Josh and Dan swore sleepily, and long before the sun flashed down into our eyes, a mountaineer, Melissa's black-headed sire, brought us minnows which he had insisted on catching without help. Willie wondered at his anxious spirit of lonely accommodation, but it was no secret to the rest of us. The chances were that he was a moonshiner, and that he had a " still " within a mile of our camp—perhaps within a hundred yards; for moonshine stills are always located on little running streams like the one into which we dipped our heads that morning.

After breakfast, we went down that shaded little stream into the Breaks, where, æons ago, the majestic Cumberland met its volcanic conqueror, and, after a heaving conflict, was tumbled head and shoulders to the lower earth, to let the pent-up waters rush through its shattered ribs, and where the Big Sandy grinds through them to-day, with a roar of freedom that once must have shaken the stars. It was ideal—sun, wind, rock, and stream. The water was a bit milky; there were eddies and pools, in sunlight and in shadow, and our bait, for a wonder, was perfect—chubs, active cold-water chubs and military minnows — sucker-shaped little fellows, with one brilliant crimson streak from gill to base of tail. And we did steady, faithful work —all of us—including Tiger, who, as Willie said, was a " fisher-dog to beat the band." But is there any older and sadder tale for the sportsman than to learn, when he has reached one happy hunting-ground, that the game is on another, miles away? Thus the Indian's idea of heaven sprang! For years and years Josh and I had been planning to get to the Breaks. For years we had fished the three forks of the Cumberland, over in Kentucky, with brilliant success, and the man who had been to the Breaks always smiled indulgently when we told our tales, and told, in answer, the marvellous things possible in the wonderful Breaks. Now we were at the Breaks, and no sooner there than we were ready, in great disgust, to get away. We investigated. There had been a drought, two years before, and the mountaineers had sledged the bass under the rocks and had slaughtered them. There had been saw-mills up the river and up its tributaries, and there had been dynamiting. We found catfish a-plenty, but we were not after catfish. We wanted that king of mountain waters, the black bass, and we wanted him to run from one pound to five pounds in weight and to fight, like the devil that he is, in the clear cold waters of the Cumberland. Nobody showed disappointment more bitter than Tiger. To say that Tiger was eager and expectant is to underrate that game little sport's intelligence and his power to catch moods from his master. At first he sat on the rocks, with every shining tooth in his head a finished cameo of expectant delight, and he watched the lines shaking in the eddies as he would watch a hole for a rat, or another dog for a fight. When the line started cutting through the water and the musical hum of the reel rose, Tiger knew as well as his master just what was happening.

"Let him run, Dan," he would gurgle, delightedly. We all knew plainly that that was what he said. "Give him plenty of line. Don't strike yet—not yet. Don't you know that he's just running for a rock? Now he's swallowing the minnow—head first. Off he goes again— now's your time, man, now—wow!"

When the strike came and the line got taut and the rod bent, Tiger would begin to leap and bark at the water's edge. As Dan reeled in and the fish would flash into the air, Tiger would get frantic. When his master played a bass and the fish cut darting circles forward and back, with the tip of the rod as a centre for geo- metrical evolutions, Tiger would have sprung into the water, if he had not known better. And when the bass was on the rocks, Tiger sprang for him and brought him to his master, avoid- ing the hook as a wary lad will look out for the sharp horns of a mud-cat. But the bass were all little fellows, and Tiger gurgled his disgust most plainly.

That night, Josh and I comforted ourselves, and made Dan and Willie unhappy, with tales of what we had done in the waters of the Cum- berland — sixty bass in one day — four four- pounders in two hours, not to mention one little whale that drew the scales down to the five- pound notch three hours after I had him from the water. We recalled—he and I—how we had paddled, dragged, and lifted a clumsy ca- noe, for four days, down the wild and beautiful

Clinch (sometimes we had to go ahead and build canals through the ripples), shooting happy, blood-stirring rapids, but catching no fish, and how, down that river, we had foolishly done it again. This was the third time we had been enticed away from the Cumberland, and then and there we resolved to run after the gods of strange streams no more. Fish stories followed. Dan recalled how Cecil Rhodes got his start in South Africa, illustrating thereby the speed of the shark. Rhodes was poor, but he brought to a speculator news of the Franco-Prussian War in a London newspaper of a date five days later than the speculator's mail. The two got a corner on some commodity and made large money. Rhodes had got his paper from the belly of a shore-cast shark that had beaten the mail steamer by five round days. That was good, and Willie thereupon told a tale that he knew to be *true*.

" You know how rapidly a bass grows? "

We did not know.

" You know how a bass will use the same hole year after year? "

That we did know.

" Well, I caught a yearling once, and I bet a man that he would grow six inches in a year. To test it, I tied a little tin whistle to his tail. A year later we went and fished for him. The second day I caught him." Willie knocked the top-ashes from his pipe and puffed silently.

" Well? " we said.

Willie edged away out of reach, speaking softly.

" That tin whistle had grown to a fog-horn." We spared him, and he quickly turned to a po-etico-scientific dissertation on birds and flowers in the Blue-grass and in the mountains, surprising us. He knew, positively, what even the great Mr. Burroughs did not seem to know a few years ago, that the shrike—the butcher-bird —impales mice as well as his feathered fellows on thorns, having found a nest in a thorn-tree up in the Blue-grass which was a ghastly, aërial, Indian-like burying-place for two mice and twenty song-sparrows. So, next day, Willie and I turned unavailingly to Melissa, whom we saw but once speeding through the weeds along the creek bank for home and, with success, to Nature; while the indefatigable Josh and Dan and Tiger whipped the all but responseless waters once more.

We reached camp at sunset—dispirited all. Tiger refused to be comforted until we turned loose two big catfish in a pool of the minnow branch and gave him permission to bring them out. With a happy wow Tiger sprang for the outsticking point of a horn and with a mad yelp sprang clear of the water. With one rub of his pricked nose against the bank, he jumped again. Wherever the surface of the water rippled, he made a dash, nosing under the grassy clumps where the fish tried to hide. Twice he got one clear of the water, but it was hard to hold to the slippery, leathery skins. In ten minutes he laid both, gasping, on the bank.

Next morning we struck camp. Willie said he would go on ahead and let down the fence —which was near Melissa's cabin. He was sitting on the fence, with a disconsolate pipe between his teeth, when we rattled and shook over the stony way up the creek—sitting alone. Yet he confessed. He had had a brief farewell with Melissa. What did she say?"

"She said she was sorry we were going," said modest Willie, but he did not say what he said; and he lifted the lid of the typewriter case, the label of which was slowly emptying to a sad and empty lie.

"Thus pass the flowers," he said, with a last backward look to the log-cabin and the black-haired, blackberry-stained figure watching at the corner. "Such is life—a lick and a promise, and then no more." The wagon passed under the hill, and Melissa, the maid of the Breaks, had come and Melissa had gone forever.

Only next day, however—for such, too, is life—the aching void in Willie's imagination, and what he was pleased to call his heart, was nicely filled again.

That night we struck the confluence of Russell's Fork and the Pound, where, under wide sycamores, the meeting of swift waters had lifted from the river-beds a high breach of white sand and had considerately overspread it with piles of dry drift-wood. The place was ideal— why not try it there? The freedom of gypsies was ours, and we did. There was no rain in the sky, so we pitched no tent, but slept on the sand, under the leaves of the sycamore, and, by the light of the fire, we solaced ourselves with the cheery game of " draw." It was a happy night, in spite of Willie's disappointment with the game. He played with sorrow, and to his cost. He was accustomed to table stakes; he did not know how to act on a modest fifty-cent limit, being denied the noble privilege of " bluff."

" I was playing once with a fellow I knew slightly," he said, reminiscently and as though for self-comfort, " and with two others whom I didn't know at all. The money got down between me and one of the strangers, and when the other stranger dealt the last hand my suspicions were aroused. I picked up my hand. He had dealt me a full house — three aces and a pair. I made up my mind that he had dealt his confederate four of a kind, and do you know what I did? I discarded the pair and actually caught the remaining ace. When it came to a show-down he had four deuces. I scooped in all the gold, pushed over to my acquaintance what he had lost—in their presence—and left the table." Perhaps it was just as well that we denied Willie his own game, and thus kept him shorn of his strength.

Next day was hard, faithful, fruitless—Josh and I fishing up-stream and Dan and Willie wading down the " Pound "—and we came in at dark, each pair with a few three-quarter pound bass, only Willie having had a bigger catch. They had struck a mill, Dan said, which Willie entered — reappearing at once and silently setting his rod, and going back again, to reappear no more. Dan found him in there with his catch — a mountain maid, fairer even than Melissa, and *she was running the mill.*

Dan had hard work to get him away, but Willie came with a silent purpose that he un-veiled at the camp-fire—when he put his rod to-gether. He was done fishing for fish; the proper study of mankind being man, his proper study, next day, would be the maid of the mill, and he had forged his plan. He would hire a mule, put on jean trousers, a slouch hat, and a homespun skirt, buy a bag of corn, and go to the mill. When that bag was ground, he would go out and buy another. All his life he had wanted to learn the milling business, and, while we fished, he would learn. But we had had enough, and were stern. We would move on from those hard-fished, fishless waters next day. In silent acquiescence Willie made for the wooden box and its fluid consolation, and when he was through with label and jug, the tale of the altered title was doubly true.

" No gal."

It takes very little to make humor in the woods.

We did move on, but so strong is hope and so powerful the ancient hunting instinct in us all, that we stopped again and fished again, with the same result, in the Pound. Something was wrong. Human effort could do no more. So, after sleep on a high hill, through a windstorm, it was home with us, and with unalterable decision this time we started, climbing hills, sliding down them, tooling around the edge of steep cliffs—sun-baked, bewhiskered, and happy, in spite of the days of hard, hard luck.

Tiger rode on the camp-chest just in front

of me. Going up a hill the wagon jolted, and the dog slipped and fell between the wheels. The hind wheel, I saw, would pass over the dog's body, and if Tiger had been a child, I couldn't have been more numb with horror. The wheel ran squarely over him, crushing him into the sand. The little fellow gave one short, brave, surprised yelp. Then he sprang up and trotted after us — unhurt. It was a miracle, easier to believe for the reason that that particular hind wheel was a wheel of kindly magic. Only an hour before it had run squarely over a little haversack in which were a bottle, a pipe, and other fragile things, and not a thing was broken. I do not believe it would have been possible so to arrange the contents and let the wheel run over it as harmlessly again.

Another night, another hot day, and another, and we were tooling down into the beautiful little valley, toward the sunset and " The Gap " —toward razor, bathtub, dinner, Willie's guitar and darky songs, and a sound, sweet sleep in each man's own bed—through dreams of green hills, gray walls, sharp peaks, and clear, swift waters, from which no fish flashed to seductive fly or crimson-streaked minnow. But with all the memories, no more of the Breaks for Josh or Dan or for me; and no more, doubtless, for Willie, though Melissa be there waiting for him, and though the other maid, with the light of mountain waters in her eyes, be dreaming of him at her mill.

After the gods of strange streams we would run no more.

THE END